MW01603015

FIRST TO DOUGH

RAISED AND GLAZED COZY MYSTERIES,
BOOK 13

EMMA AINSLEY

SUMMER PRESCOTT BOOKS PUBLISHING

CHAPTER ONE

"I can't believe we pulled this off," Myra Sawyer said. She stood next to Ruby Cobb at the prep table in the kitchen of Dogwood Donuts. Maggie Sharpe, the owner of the donut shop, smiled at her from across the room. She felt a little swell of pride when she looked at Myra, who had come to her as a desperate young woman and was now anything but.

"You haven't pulled anything off just yet," Orson Hawley muttered. He carried a basket of fresh strawberries over to the baker's table and plopped them down heavily. Maggie felt the weight of the table shift. She eyed Orson, wondering what had him all worked up so early in the morning.

"I thought I told you to wait until someone could

help you unload those strawberries," Ruby scolded him. "I wanted Jake to help you."

"Yeah, well, Jake is with Flo right now," Orson said. Maggie detected a slight roll of his eyes. Like Myra, Jake Jenkins was a young person who had come into their lives in need and had turned out to be a friend and an amazingly helpful coworker. Florence Johnson was a new friend, too, and she had quickly become part of the donut shop family. After an unfortunate situation with her uncle, Flo had chosen to sell the diner she shared with him and move on to bigger and better things.

"You still don't need to lift everything by yourself," Maggie said.

"All by myself is right," he muttered then turned to face her. His height and ire towered over her. "Let us not forget that until young Jake came around, I was the one and only man around these parts," he said. "My bones might be old, but until they're in the ground, I will continue to lift the heavy stuff and open the doors for you and the other ladies here."

"You're right, Orson," Ruby said. She walked across the floor and handed him a small bowl of his favorite apple slaw. "Why don't you taste test this new and improved recipe and tell me what you think?"

"Now you're just placating me," Orson grumbled. He took the bowl out of her hand and sank onto the wooden stool next to the baker's table. His frown reminded Maggie of her son Bradley when he pouted at age three. Something was bothering him but trying to figure out what it was would be like pulling teeth.

"I'm not placating you," Ruby said gently. "I want you to take your time between heavy loads, yes. But I do trust your opinions on the flavors and recipes I experiment with. And that's why I'm asking you what you think."

He took a bite of the apple slaw and his frown melted into a smile. "What did you do differently?"

"I take it you like this version better?" Maggie asked.

Orson turned his attention to her. "Have you tasted this? It's heaven in a bowl!"

Ruby laughed out loud. She circled his shoulders in a hug. "I added creamy Greek yogurt to the dressing and switched apple varieties. Those are Gala apples," she said, peering over his shoulder. "Oh, and this version has cranberries and sliced almonds."

"It's perfect," Orson said. "Absolutely perfect. You should replace the old recipe with this. Replace it just like everything else gets replaced."

"What do you mean by that?" Maggie asked,

concerned by his mood swings. "Have I replaced something you wanted to keep around?"

"You've done nothing wrong." Orson sighed and took another bite of the slaw. "The slaw needs replacing. Ruby, you did a fine job."

"Thank you." Ruby patted his shoulder and headed back to the prep table. "I'd like to debut the new recipe this weekend."

"I still can't believe the city and the chamber of commerce worked so quickly to help this whole event launch," Myra said finally, having not uttered a word about Orson or the new recipe.

Ruby nodded. "It's pretty unheard of, but the town of Dogwood Mountain has always supported local businesses," she said. "Anything that helps bring in more tourism is a plus."

"It's nice to have so much local support," Maggie agreed.

"I have one question for you two," Orson announced.

"Which two?" Ruby asked.

"You two," he said, pointing at Maggie and Ruby. He gave Myra a look like there was no way he could possibly be speaking to her. "Why did you order so many strawberries?"

"We're making a new fritter for the spring fling,"

Maggie answered. "I'm working on finalizing it now, so we can make a batch to try out."

"Don't we make apple fritters?" he asked. "Why fix something that isn't broken and why add new fruit to the mix? Are the old things just not good enough anymore?"

"Orson, really!" Myra snapped and stormed out of the kitchen door.

Maggie and Ruby shared a glance as Orson stared at them, waiting for an answer.

"We do make apple fritters, and we will keep making them. However, we're going to try out a strawberry cream cheese fritter with a honey-cinnamon glaze for the spring fling," Maggie said. "But Orson, none of that is important right now. Do you want to tell us what's going on? Did you and Myra get into a fight about something?"

"I'm fine, she's fine, Brooks is fine, everything is just fine fine fine." He bobbled his head around as he spoke. "Now, more about these fritters. Is the cream cheese inside?"

Maggie looked at Ruby with wide eyes and only as best friends can, they decided silently not to push Orson.

"The inside will be stuffed with a strawberry cream cheese, yes," Ruby said.

Orson's eyes widened. "And instead of our regular glaze, it'll be cinnamon and honey?" he asked.

"That's exactly right. We should have a batch ready in about an hour if you want to be the first to try them." Maggie smiled.

"I'd like that. Thanks for taking the time to consider me," Orson said before heading out of the kitchen.

As the door swung behind him, Maggie caught his gruff reply to Myra who was standing behind the counter. She had quietly asked him to unlock the front door as it was time for the shop to open. Orson responded with, "Oh, now you need me for something. Must be nice to get what you want all the time."

Just as the swinging door came to a stop, Maggie peered through the small window to see Orson walk away. Myra, shoulders slumped, went to unlock the front door herself. Something was clearly going on between them and it didn't appear to be anything good.

CHAPTER TWO

"Maggie? There's someone out here who wants to speak with you." Myra popped her head through the kitchen doorway an hour later.

"Coming," Maggie said. Despite leaving Myra in charge of the public relations part of the upcoming spring fling they were hosting, many local business owners had visited her at the donut shop. She expected to see another one of them with a demand or specific request. There was something about speaking to the owner of a business that made people feel more official, so while she couldn't blame them, she didn't want to take away anything from all of Myra's hard work.

For the most part, the requests were simple to solve, and Myra took care of the situation easily.

However, the demands Maggie detested were those that involved bumping another business from a favored position in the parking lot. Three times already, she had been offered a small bribe to kick her food truck out of its position directly in front of the donut shop. There was no way she'd put Myra in the middle of that.

She was glad to see Pam Carter, a member of the Dogwood Mountain City Council smiling back at her when she emerged from the kitchen. "Good morning, Pam," she said brightly.

"Good morning," Pam said. "I just wanted to stop by and make sure everything was set and ready to go for this weekend. I can't tell you how many of my fellow council members are excited about what you all have put together in such a short amount of time."

Maggie smiled and nodded in Myra's direction. "There's the person you owe your gratitude to," she said. "Myra has worked tirelessly to put this whole thing together."

"Well, then," Pam said and turned her attention to Myra. "Thank you for your diligence and your dedication to the town of Dogwood Mountain."

"Yes, of course. I'm happy to help. Can I get you something from the display case?" Myra asked. She blushed as she spoke.

"On the house," Maggie added.

Pam smiled and leaned forward as if she was about to share a deep, dark secret. "Do you have any special new recipes back there you can share with me?" she asked. Her tight, gray curls bounced as she spoke.

"You know, sort of a preview to what you will offer?"

"How much time do you have?" Maggie asked with a chuckle.

"Oh, I have all morning." Pam waved her hand in the air and giggled.

"Well, then please have a seat back there in the corner and let us bring you a sampling of our new flavors," Maggie said. "Just give me a moment to put together a tray for you."

"On it," Myra said. She disappeared to the back and left Maggie with the hungry city council member.

"Why don't I bring you some coffee while you wait?" Maggie suggested. Pam smiled and found her way to a booth on the far side of the shop. She seemed to understand that Maggie was in no hurry to advertise her offer of free samples to anyone else.

After she delivered Pam's coffee, Maggie walked past the large front windows and gazed out in the parking lot. Flo's recently purchased and remodeled food truck sat next to the donut shop's food truck under the tall marquee sign near the road. In some ways, the younger woman reminded her of Myra when they'd first met, although Flo was much older and didn't quite have the same mind for business as Myra.

Maggie could see Jake, the youngest and newest member of the donut shop crew, moving around and following Flo's orders. Soon enough, she would have to hire someone to help her out, but for now, Maggie was happy to lend Jake to her while she got things up and running.

While she was still looking outside, an older pickup truck sped off of the road and veered into the parking lot. The truck rounded the lot in a wide circle, barely missing the parked cars near the front. It turned and came back around a second time, heading for the parked food trucks. The truck screeched to a halt just a few feet from Flo's truck and sat still for a moment, revving the engine before shifting into reverse. White smoke rose from the tires before the driver shifted into drive and tore back out of the parking lot and out into the street.

"What in the heck was that all about?" Myra asked. She had returned to the front counter holding a tray filled with goodies for Pam.

"I don't know, but I have half a mind to call the chief of police," Maggie said. She pulled her phone out of her pocket and tapped the screen. The police chief's number was number five on her speed dial. As her boyfriend, she didn't feel uncomfortable in the least calling to tell him about an erratic driver.

"I don't think you need to call," Myra said. She pointed down the street at the familiar police cruiser speeding down the road after the pickup truck.

Maggie smiled and leaned against the counter. For a moment, all she could picture was Brett in his police uniform, but Myra's voice interrupted her thoughts.

"Mrs. Carter? I thought you wanted to try our special recipes?" Myra said, backing away from Pam's table.

Maggie turned and watched as a pale-faced Pam Carter headed straight for the door. She muttered something about a forgotten appointment and practically ran out into the parking lot.

Maggie watched in shock as the older woman raced from the parking lot nearly as fast as the light blue pickup had gone.

"What the heck is happening?" Myra asked again.

Maggie shook her head. "I haven't got a clue," she admitted. "Whatever it is, I sure hope that it has nothing to do with the spring fling."

"What's happening is that you offered your fancy strawberry fritter to someone before I got the chance to try it. Is nothing sacred anymore?" Orson bellowed from behind the counter. "A guy goes to the storeroom to organize for an hour and comes out being pushed to the side once again."

"That's enough," Myra said. "You can be as upset with me as you want but you have no right to treat Maggie or anyone else that way."

"Okay, you two. Would one of you like to share with me what's going on?" Maggie asked with her hands on her hips.

"She will tell you when she's ready, apparently." Orson huffed and turned on his heel.

Maggie turned to Myra with a confused look on her face. "Is he okay? Are you?" she asked.

"I'm great, and he'll be fine, too. But he better stop acting so rudely before I call Gretchen," Myra warned. "If she found out how he was acting, she'd put a stop to it."

Gretchen LeClair was Orson's girlfriend of sorts. They kept their relationship quiet, but it was always easy to see they cared deeply for one another. She tended to balance out his grumpiness. Maggie thought maybe she needed to call Gretchen herself to get the details about whatever it was that was going on. She didn't want to pry into the lives of her employees, but it made for long days on the job when they weren't getting along. She didn't have it half as bad as Myra, though, who rented a room from Orson. She had to work with him and live with him. Maggie didn't envy the young woman for a moment.

"If there's anything I can do, let me know. But you both have to keep whatever this is at home. We can't go running around this place like it's our living room."

"You're right. I'll talk to him, and I promise I'll do better, too. Now, what should I do with all of this?" Myra asked. She held up the tray she had prepared for Pam Carter.

Maggie looked around for a moment. The dining room was filled with customers already enjoying their breakfast and coffee, and thankfully, none of them were paying attention to what was going on. "Throw a clean towel over it and give it to me," she said. "I'll take a walk out to the parking lot and see if Flo and Jake are hungry. And you can stop by all the tables and make sure every single person in here is as happy as can be. If they aren't, you offer them a free donut or coffee. Understand?"

"Yes, ma'am." Myra nodded. She handed over the tray and dashed off to a table.

CHAPTER THREE

Maggie pushed through the front doors with her back. She carried the tray over the sidewalk and between parked cars. She reached the food truck and tapped the side lightly with her elbow.

"Flo," she called out. "Jake?"

"Oh, Maggie!" Flo opened the order window. "I didn't know you were there. Is everything okay?"

"That's what I was going to ask you. That truck came awfully close to you guys out here."

"No kidding. I'm just thankful we happened to have stepped inside the truck or who knows what could have happened?" Flo put her hand over her heart. "Hey, what's under the towel?"

"Oh, just some samples of what we plan on offering this weekend. We had a member of the city council come in and request a taste test, but she tore out of here right after that pickup truck came through."

"I hope everything is okay with her, but I won't deny any samples." Flo grinned. She disappeared from the window and reappeared holding the food truck door open a second later. "Why don't you come in, and we can chat for a second?"

Maggie handed the tray to Flo and stepped up inside the truck. Unlike her own, nearly every square inch of available space held some function or another. "You don't have a bathroom in here, do you?"

Flo shook her head. "No, I sure don't," she said. "But we do have an extra fryer over there in the corner and a full-size grill."

Maggie nodded. "I suppose that's more important for an actual restaurant food truck," she said. "Do you have your menu ready for this weekend?"

Flo smiled. "Since this is sort of my debut, whatever I have is what I'm going to debut with." She chuckled. "Ruby has been amazing with her advice. Myra and I are still working on my business plan, and she is incredible, too. I can't thank you enough." Jake turned around from the sink where he was washing a large pan and cleared his throat. "You, too, Jake. You're priceless to me, too."

Maggie clapped her hands and giggled. "Well-timed, Jake," she said. "And I'm so glad you have had the help. I'm just happy to see you out here making a go of it."

Flo picked up a small whiteboard and handed it to Maggie. "Ruby helped me to plan a small menu of offerings, along with a daily special," she said. "I spent so much time trying to figure out how I was going to offer the same menu we had at Pop's, and I think I ended up getting myself all twisted and feeling down about things."

"I did the same thing with our food truck at first," Maggie said. "I wanted to recreate the donut shop but eventually I realized that I didn't have to do that."

Flo lifted the towel from the tray and eyed all the treats. "I just have to keep reminding myself that this food truck isn't the diner. It's okay to be different."

Maggie nodded. "Are you all stocked up and ready for this weekend?"

"With Jake's help, yes," she said and glanced at him. "I mean that. But I know I'm going to have to hire someone else soon, especially once I figure out where I'm going to park on a more permanent basis." She shrugged and turned her attention to the creamy apple slaw Myra had included on the tray.

"Wait, what do you mean about a more permanent

17

place?" Maggie asked as Jake headed out of the food truck and back to the donut shop.

"Well, that's one part of the business plan we haven't quite figured out yet," Flo admitted.

Maggie accepted the bottle of water Flo offered her and twisted the cap off. "That part is simple to solve. You park here and your customers can use this parking lot. Your hours of operation are almost the opposite of ours. I will furnish you with a key to the building so you can use the facilities as needed."

"Maggie," Flo said. "You've already been extremely generous. I can't expect you to extend that sort of invitation to me on top of everything else. I'm looking for a lot of my own, it's just that with the debut and stuff, I haven't been able to get out to look as much as I wanted to."

"It's my pleasure, truly," Maggie said. "The offer stands if you want to stay here until you find the right place."

Flo dropped her head and shook it side to side. "You are too kind," she said. "I've never met anyone like you before."

Maggie waved her hand in the air. "Oh, trust me," she said. "I might be kind, but I also have an ulterior motive. The more traffic you bring to my location, the more people who buy donuts."

"Or so we hope," Flo said.

"Who knows? Maybe there will be events in the future that we both attend," Maggie said. "I don't have a lot of focus on the food truck right now but watching you sure is inspiring me."

"I'm up for anything," Flo said. She picked up one of the new strawberry fritters and tore a piece of it off. "This is different."

"Try it and let me know what you think."

Flo complied. Her eyes widened when she tasted it. "Cream cheese?"

"Honey, cinnamon, and cream cheese," Maggie said. "What do you think?"

She popped another large piece into her mouth. "I think I'm going to have to double my time at the gym," she said. "I've never had anything more delicious! You guys are all so creative."

Maggie left her with the tray of goods and headed back across the parking lot to the donut shop. She noted more vacant spaces than she had seen a few minutes before. One more car was in the parking lot, the same cruiser she had seen taking off after the light blue pickup truck a little while before.

"Chief." Maggie nodded to Brett when he opened the door for her.

"Chief? What happened to Brett?" he asked. He

spoke close to her ear. "Don't tell me you're still mad about making you watch that movie last night?"

"That was the longest, most boring thing on the planet, but no, I'm not mad at you." She breezed past him and headed for the counter. "I'm not angry at you at all," she said with an unconvincing smirk. "You are the chief of police, and you are clearly on duty."

Brett gazed at her for a moment. "And clearly, you will be choosing the movie next time." He grinned but it quickly turned into a frown. "Actually, I am here on official business, but I'll take something to drink if you don't mind," he said.

Maggie looked at him carefully, wondering what the official business was. "What would you like?"

"How about something with chocolate in it?" Brett asked. "Maybe a mocha cappuccino. I could use the extra kick this morning."

"Do you want a snack to go along with that? I have some special strawberry fritters in the back," Maggie said. "They're a test run for the festival this weekend and they'd probably go really well with the mocha."

"You twisted my arm." He smiled.

Maggie moved to the back and headed straight for the cooling rack where the rest of the fritters were.

"How's Brett?" Ruby asked her.

"Good, I guess. He says he's here on official business but placed an order first. Hopefully whatever he has to say isn't bad news about the spring fling."

"Stop worrying. This weekend is going to be amazing."

"Yeah," Maggie mumbled, not entirely certain. She headed back to the front with the fritter on a plate.

"This looks amazing," Brett said. "Tell me all about it."

Myra handed the mocha cappuccino to Maggie, who passed it off to Brett. She told him everything she could about the fritter and then stared at him with her hands on her hips. "Now it's your turn to tell me all about why you're here."

Brett sipped the hot drink and set it back on the counter. "The pickup that sped through here not too long ago," he said in a low voice. "Did you recognize the truck?"

"How did you even know I knew about it?"

"Because you pay attention to everything." Brett rolled his eyes. "Did you recognize it or not?"

Maggie shook her head. "I don't think I've seen it before," she said. "And I know for a fact that I've never seen the same truck careening around my parking lot before today."

Brett's face fell. "I was hoping you might know a little about the truck or the driver," he said. "I chased them for a while, and then they veered off the road and disappeared."

"Do you think they're from around here?"

"I don't think so," Brett answered.

"Did you happen to see any tags?" she asked.

"Hey," Brett said. "Exactly who is the police officer here?"

Maggie smiled despite herself. "I just wondered if you knew for sure if they were from out of state."

"I didn't see any tags on the truck at all," he said. "That's one of the reasons I want to speak with the driver."

"And what are the other reasons?" Maggie asked.

"Well, the main reason is the sinking feeling in my gut that whoever is in that pickup is up to no good," he admitted.

CHAPTER FOUR

On Thursday night, after the donut shop closed, Maggie ran home just long enough to change out of her work shoes and jeans. She put on a comfortable pair of yoga pants and a sweatshirt and dashed back to the shop to meet Ruby who had done the very same thing. When she returned, she found three vendors already setting up their tents for the following morning.

The local bookstore owner, Faylene Larabee, was among them. She'd been directing two young men when Maggie walked up to her vendor space. Maggie waited patiently while the men listened to Faylene's orders. They worked to put up a large outdoor canopy tent. Faylene helped place books on the wooden shelves they set up inside the tent walls.

"This is my kind of display," Maggie said. "All I need is my favorite coffee mug and a comfy chair."

"I'll have chairs set up tomorrow," Faylene said with a wide grin. "I'll look to you to keep the hot drinks coming for my patrons."

"And what about you?" Maggie asked. "What's your hot drink of choice?"

Faylene leaned against the side of the truck one of the young men drove. She pulled a flyer out of her coat pocket and flipped it open. "I was looking over this pamphlet of your specials and I find myself quite intrigued by this honey nut coffee offering. Why haven't you made this for me during one of our coffee chats?"

Maggie laughed. She had come to adore the coffee chats with the bookstore owner. "This is Ruby's special concoction developed in honor of the spring fling. I didn't even know about it until a week ago."

"I look forward to it," Faylene said. "Now, are you going to fill me in on all of the gossip when this weekend is over?"

"You better believe it," Maggie promised. She left Faylene with a promise for coffee the coming week and headed back to the donut shop. When she opened the front door, she was surprised to see Flo setting up cartons of food on the front table. "What's this?"

"Dinner." Flo smiled. "Ruby and I worked out a bargain. I've got dinner, and she promised me all of the coffee and pastries I can stand."

"Sounds like a plan to me," Maggie said. She was eager to slide into one of the chairs and begin her feast.

Ruby took her seat and Maggie followed suit. She opened the Styrofoam container and smiled. Flo had prepared a chopped sirloin sandwich with au jus. "This smells divine."

"I'm glad you approve," Flo said. "This is one of my standard menu items. It was one of the best sellers at Pop's." Flo pulled out her chair and smiled as she sank into it.

Ruby raised her foam cup in the air. "To 'The Diner!'"

"I really love how simple the name is," Maggie said.

"Yup!" Flo agreed. "It fits, it tells the customer exactly what to expect, and I don't have to change the paint on the food truck."

"Hey, look who's here," Ruby said. She pointed out the window.

Brett pulled up in front of the donut shop in his

25

personal vehicle. Maggie watched as he stepped out dressed in jeans and a pullover.

"I wonder what he's doing here," she said and rose to unlock the door for him.

Brett walked in without a word to Maggie. He headed straight for the table and took a seat. "I'm sorry to interrupt, ladies," he said. He appeared to be out of breath.

"Would you like something to eat, Chief?" Flo asked. She rose halfway out of her chair.

"No, no," Brett said, waving her back down. "I'm not here for something to eat. I just came from the station. I wanted to stop in and let you all know something before you hear from someone else."

"Oh no. What's going on?" Ruby asked.

"Councilwoman Pam Carter is missing," he said. "Or at least, no one has seen or heard from her since this morning when she took off from here."

"She's missing? Are you sure?" Maggie stood up and headed for the counter. Despite his comments, she decided Brett could use a cup of coffee.

"It's too early yet to declare her a missing person, but her family hasn't had any contact and they can't reach her on her cell phone," he said. Maggie set the coffee in front of him. "Thank you."

"Should we cancel the spring fling?" Ruby asked. "Is that why you're really here?"

Brett sipped his coffee and shook his head. "No, I don't think that's necessary at all," he said. "I think that would be the very definition of jumping the gun."

"But it sort of feels like we should be celebrating and having fun at the festival. How are we supposed to do that, when one of the people who helped make this possible is missing?" Maggie asked.

Brett nodded. "I understand, but if you stop all the work you've been doing, and Pam pops back up, then you will regret not being ready for the weekend. I know it's hard to hear, and even if it's not official yet, we do have people keeping an eye out for her."

"He's right, Maggie," Ruby said. "Pam might have gotten busy with something and forgot to tell her family she had some important meeting for work."

"Yeah, maybe." Maggie didn't want to put a stop to all their hard work, but the idea that Pam had simply forgotten to tell her family she had plans, didn't sit quite right with her.

CHAPTER FIVE

Maggie woke up earlier than normal the next morning. Despite still not hearing anything about Pam, her mind buzzed with excitement about the coming day. She showered quickly and dressed in her newest work smock and a pair of comfortable jeans. She slipped her feet into her boots but grabbed her favorite memory foam slippers and stuffed them into her bag, just in case. There was no way she would traipse around in them publicly, but sometimes a girl needed cozy footwear to get through a busy day.

Headlights streamed through her dining room windows. Ruby pulled her truck in front of the garage and parked. Through the window, Maggie could see her stretch her arms high above her head when she stepped out of the driver's door.

"You're here earlier than I expected," Maggie said as she opened the back door and turned on the porch light. She had invited Ruby, Orson, and Myra to park at her house over the weekend. As long as the weather held, the walk to the donut shop could be made in a matter of minutes. She had a feeling the alley behind the donut shop, where they normally parked, would be filled with vehicles.

"I couldn't sleep," Ruby said. "I think I'm a little too wired about this morning."

"Same here," Maggie admitted. "Are you ready to head over? We can walk together."

"Sounds good to me, but I'm going to grab my coat out of the backseat, and I suggest you run back inside and grab one for yourself," Ruby said. "It's pretty chilly out here."

Maggie left her in the yard and headed back for her favorite coat and her bag. She pulled a sweatshirt off the hook and slipped it over her head on her way out the door. The morning air was cool enough, but she had seen the forecast for the evening, and a sweatshirt might not be enough.

"Ready?" Ruby asked when Maggie emerged from the house.

"Let's go," Maggie said. She tucked her coat over

her bag and danced around the driveway. "Are we ready? Yes, we're ready!"

"Someone is in a good mood." Ruby chuckled.

Jake opened the walk-through door to the garage and waved. "Did I miss something?" he asked with a smile.

"Nope, it's just going to be a great day," Maggie said. "Are you ready to go? Want to walk with us?"

Jake shook his head. "No, I need a few more minutes, but I'll be along soon," he said and shut the door.

They walked out of the yard and down the road. "That's got to be one of the first times I have seen that boy smile," Ruby said when they were far enough away to be out of earshot.

"He has been warming up more and more," Maggie said.

"Are you okay with him staying in the garage for a while longer?" Ruby asked. "I've wanted to ask you that for a little while, but it never seems like the right time."

"I'm just fine with him staying around for a long while," Maggie said. "But he's told me he plans to get a place of his own soon. I think that's one of the reasons he's been asking for so many hours lately."

"He's looking ahead to the future," Ruby said as

they walked. "That's so terrific. He's come such a long way."

Maggie started to comment, but she heard the low rumble of an engine as they neared the end of the road. "Hold on," she said to Ruby. The trees at the end of the upcoming alley blocked her view.

"That sounds close," Ruby said. "It sounds a little familiar, too."

"It's just idling in the road," Maggie said. "There's no traffic, so he can't be waiting to turn."

Ruby held her arm in front of Maggie. "Maybe we should go the other way," she said. "After yesterday with the truck in the parking lot."

As soon as she got the words out, the engine revved up. They were suddenly caught in the vehicle's high beams. "Watch out!" Maggie pulled Ruby into the trees. She looked up at the vehicle, a pickup truck, as it careened past them. The truck reached the end of the alley, then whipped into a nearby drive, then pulled back out again.

"He's coming back this way!" Ruby shouted and pulled Maggie with her between two trees. The pickup truck crept down the alley revving up the engine and waiting. A moment later the truck slammed into drive and fishtailed toward them. Maggie screamed and hid her face against the tree.

The truck raced past them and swerved back out onto the road. It was gone in a cloud of dust and smoke.

"What the heck was that?" Jake yelled and came running toward them.

"Jake, get out of the way in case he comes back," Maggie shouted.

"We're less than a block from the donut shop," Ruby said. "Jake, go back to Maggie's and get my truck. There's a hideaway key under the front wheel well. Come and pick us up and we'll ride back and forth together today."

"I'll be back as soon as I can," he said. Maggie kept herself pressed against the tree.

"We have to call Brett," she said. "That has to be the same truck we saw yesterday."

"I would lay down money that it was," Ruby said. "Same truck. Same driver. Only this time it seems they were after us specifically."

Maggie's face was pale as she turned to Ruby. "I don't think I'll ever forget that sound for the rest of my life."

CHAPTER SIX

"So, let me ask again." Brett stood in the kitchen of the donut shop less than an hour later. "You're sure it was the same truck both times and that you don't recognize it at all?"

"I've never seen that truck before," Maggie replied.

Ruby shook her head. "Me, either. And I think I would recognize the sound of it, you know? That engine is pretty distinct."

"Did the one that came racing through the parking lot yesterday sound the same?" Brett asked.

Maggie nodded but was starting to get annoyed with having to repeat herself. "It sounded exactly the same," she said. "If I hadn't seen it up close, I would still believe it was the same truck."

"Okay," Brett said. His face was drawn into a tight frown. "Can you remember if the driver saw you two walking?"

"You mean did they purposely try to run us down?" Maggie asked. "What else could it be? First they come barreling into the parking lot like a bat out of you know what and now this? It's hard to believe there's another option."

"Honestly, I don't think they could have," Ruby said and looked at Maggie. "I don't know how they could have seen us before we sought shelter in the trees."

Maggie sighed. "She's right."

"Maybe you ought to learn how to climb one," Orson mumbled. He was seated on a stool across the baker's table where he refused to move until he heard every last bit of the conversation with Brett.

"I appreciate the help but I'm not so sure that would have done us any good," Maggie said. This was the first time he'd really spoken since his outburst with Myra. She didn't want to press his buttons.

"For the next time someone tries to run you down. If you climb the tree, they can't run you over. Anything has to be better than hoping hiding out will protect you," Orson snapped.

"I know how to climb a tree, but I don't think it would have helped us," Ruby said gently. She gave Maggie a look that said Orson was cross from worry. But Maggie knew it had to be something more than that.

"Going up a tree wouldn't have helped," Jake added. Until then, he hadn't had much to say. "If someone is really after them, I think they might go beyond using their truck."

"Do you recognize that truck from anywhere else, Jake?" Brett asked.

"I can't think of anywhere I have seen or heard that truck before," Jake said. "I'm not aware of anybody who has a light blue pickup truck."

"Alright, well." Brett straightened up. "I'm going to take my notes and run it down to my investigators. If you see any sign of that pickup, I want you to call me right away. And if you can, slow down and look for any distinctive marks on the truck. Since none of us have seen a license plate on it we don't have a lot to go on."

"I'll tell Flo the same thing," Maggie offered. "She's out there and can see a lot more than we will if we're in the kitchen."

"I can tell her," Jake said. "I'm going to head that way anyway, unless you need me."

"No, go on," Maggie said. "We're fine here."

He nodded and headed out through the kitchen door. Ruby turned her attention back to the apple slaw she was adding to the boxed lunches and Maggie resumed her work on the second set of white chocolate raspberry scones for the morning. When she was done, she checked the pans of cinnamon rolls she intended to transfer to the food truck for fast baking in the small oven.

"How long do you plan to be here today, Orson?" Ruby asked.

"Why? What are you up to?" he asked.

"Nothing, I was just thinking about the food truck," Ruby replied. "I think that two of us ought to be out there all the time. If you're going to stick around for a while that might help."

"Definitely," Maggie added. "Maybe you and Myra can work together for a little while?" She wanted to gauge his reaction to her mentioning Myra and see if she could pull anything out of him.

"How about the two of you run along to the food truck and let me have the kitchen to myself for once?"

Maggie shook her head and let out a chuckle. His reply hadn't surprised her, but it also hadn't given her anything to go on either. "Is there some reason why you don't want to work with Myra?"

Orson looked down, inhaled deeply, and set his gaze on Maggie. "I didn't say a word about her, now did I? She will be in the building with me if you two go outside. If it's me being on my own that has you upset, don't you worry... The girl can help me if you think I need it, but I won't be the one asking for it."

"The girl?" Ruby said, staring at him with her mouth open. "Since when do you call her that?"

"Since she's decided not to make me a priority in her life. And that's all I'm going to say about it. Now, I could use some peace and quiet, so unless you are asking me as your employee to work in the food truck, I'd like to get back to my job in here."

"Maggie?" Ruby looked at her.

"Thanks for the idea, Orson. I think Ruby and I will head out to the food truck for a while. If you change your mind or get bored in here, feel free to let one of us know and we can switch."

"Great. Glad I could help," he said, puffing his chest out a bit.

Ruby raised a brow. "Right, thank you, Orson," she said. "I'm going to head out there and get things going."

"I'll be right behind you with the fritter batter and cinnamon rolls," Maggie said.

She hefted a tray of unbaked cinnamon rolls from

the rack and headed out through the front. She balanced the tray while she unlocked the front door and headed out into the parking lot. She was surprised to see all of the slots were filled. Even though it wasn't quite six yet, several people were already walking around the parking lot, although she wasn't sure if they were other vendors or eager shoppers.

"Got it," Myra called out from inside the truck when Maggie approached. "I was just about to check on you guys in the kitchen."

"We were held up by a police inquisition," Maggie said wryly. "Brett took our statements about the blue pickup truck."

"Did he come up with anything? Did anyone else see it?" Myra asked.

"Aside from us, not that I know of, but I can't imagine no one else heard it," Maggie said.

"Brooks told me to call him before I leave today," Myra said. "After he heard about the truck coming back this morning, he is convinced that someone has it out for the donut shop."

"It sure seems like someone has a problem with us," Maggie agreed.

"It could be the spring fling itself," Ruby said, stepping up into the food truck. "I was just picking up around outside to make sure our area is nice and clean and every time I clean, I start overthinking."

"Don't you think we would have had more resistance before now? We've talked about this weekend for nearly a month, and advertised for nearly just as long," Maggie said. "None of the city officials seemed to think it would be a problem."

"No, but none of our city council members went missing before now," Ruby reminded her. "Has anyone heard anything about Pam Carter?"

"Brett hasn't said a word, but since it never came out that there was an official missing person's case, I just assumed she'd either turned up, or there was some other reason for her being gone."

"Yeah, that makes sense. I guess I thought you might have some inside information from Brett or something." Ruby grinned.

"Like she wouldn't share every last detail with you." Myra laughed as she got ready to go back to the donut shop.

"Hey, Myra," Ruby said just before she stepped out of the truck. "Do you know what's up with Orson lately?"

She looked down at the box she was carrying and lingered a little too long. When she looked up she gasped and dashed out of the food truck. "Look how many people are here! I'd better get to work."

Maggie and Ruby shared a look, both equally as confused as the other.

"I'm guessing they have a secret," Maggie said.

Ruby huffed. "And it seems we aren't invited to know what it is."

CHAPTER SEVEN

At just after six, the church parking lot across the street began to fill up. The pastor had been kind enough to offer it up for the festival. Maggie invited him to stop by for a free coffee and donut. She also agreed to pass out his flyers advertising the bounce house and kids' activities in the gymnasium.

"Welcome to the first ever Dogwood Mountain Spring Fling!" City Clerk Dana Perkins, called out over a loudspeaker. "We owe our thanks to Maggie and Ruby and the other good folks here at Dogwood Donuts for putting this together. We hope this will be an annual event showcasing the best Dogwood Mountain has to offer!"

Maggie applauded from the front of the food truck. Ruby remained inside to watch the mini donut machine and the deep fryer where the first strawberry fritters were sizzling.

"Make sure you visit each vendor here. Pastor Mark Jensen has activities for the kids across the street.

Hang around for lunch and even dinner with our newest merchant, Florence Johnson at The Diner. It's that food truck parked all the way over there under the donut shop sign," Dana continued. She pointed toward the sign and was quickly rewarded by a ripple of laughter from the gathered crowd.

After that, the P.A. system was returned to the mayor's car and the crowd began to mill around. Maggie watched as several high-school-age girls made a beeline for Faylene's bookstore tent. Before she returned to the food truck, she scanned the crowd for signs of Pam Carter.

"That was short and sweet," Ruby said when Maggie rejoined her inside. "Any clue why the city clerk spoke and not the mayor?"

Maggie shrugged. "I saw Mayor Savino walking around shaking hands," she said. "I have no idea why he didn't speak to the crowd."

"I guess it doesn't matter," Ruby said. "I think I'm going to let Myra and Orson know that if they want to come and walk around for a little while to check things out, they're free to do so. I don't want them to miss out on all the fun."

"I already let them both know when I went in for the fritter batter," Maggie said. "They know we have to keep up with the food production, but they're so far ahead in there that there's plenty of time for them to take a break."

Ruby pointed across the parking lot. "I guess Myra took you up on your offer. I see her and Brooks over there now."

"I expect him to show up here just about any minute now. You know he doesn't want to miss out on our food."

"Can't keep him away from the donuts with sprinkles." Ruby smiled. She opened the warming drawer under the counter and revealed about two dozen frosted and decorated mini donuts.

"Those are fantastic, but I'm shocked the icing isn't melting off," Maggie said.

"It will if I leave them in there too long," Ruby said. "But a few minutes is okay."

Before Maggie could worry any longer about the frosting, Brooks and Myra began walking toward the order window. "What can I get you to drink?" she asked.

"Drink? I don't get anything to eat?" Brooks feigned a hurt look. "Is this because…"

"Of course, you can have something to eat, silly," Myra interrupted and elbowed him in the ribs.

He looked at her and shrugged. "I was just kidding."

Ruby pulled the platter of mini donuts out from under the counter. "Will this work?"

Brooks smiled broadly. "I have a feeling you want to see me gain fifty pounds," he said. "I'm going to have to get to the gym before the…"

"Oh, wow!" Myra exclaimed, pushing herself in front of Brooks to admire the donuts. "I think I need one of these and both of us will try a chilled pear cider."

"Uhh, sure. Chilled pear cider." Brooks made a face. "Sounds delicious."

Ruby poured the pear cider into a paper cup and topped it off with a dusting of cinnamon. "Are you two okay?" She carefully placed the lid on the cup and passed it through the window to Brooks.

"I'm not sure." Brooks laughed. "Are we okay?" He looked at Myra.

She nodded quickly. "Fine, but it looks like Brett might be bearing news that will make us all not fine."

Brooks turned around and waved. "Uh oh," he

said. Brett walked down the sidewalk in front of the donut shop and stopped just outside the food truck. He said hello to Brooks and Myra and turned to the window and nodded at Maggie. "I hate to break up whatever this is, but I need to speak with Maggie and Ruby inside, if that's possible."

"Go on," Myra offered. "I'll take over here."

"You probably need to hear this, too, Brooks," Brett said. He waited while Maggie and Ruby stepped out of the food truck and headed back inside the donut shop.

"What's going on?" Ruby asked as soon as they were inside.

"I have a feeling you're about to deliver some bad news," Brooks said.

"I'm going to need you to head out as soon as we finish up here," he said. "Pam Carter's car was found in an old corn field about five miles down the road, almost to Hunter Springs."

"You said her car was found," Maggie asked. "Where was she?"

"In it," Brett said. His face was ashen. "She wasn't breathing, and while the coroner still has to take a look at her, my guess is she didn't get that way by natural causes."

CHAPTER EIGHT

Maggie hugged her middle and leaned against the baker's table. Her mind reeled. Ruby paced around in front of the sink. Orson took himself out of the kitchen and headed out to the food truck to help Myra. He said nothing and didn't act out. It seemed that he knew now wasn't the time to be difficult.

"I just don't know what to do," Maggie said at last. "Brett can't tell us whether we should stop the festival or not and I know he has work to do, but he left out of here so fast that I didn't get to ask any questions."

"I don't think he would have given you many answers, anyway," Ruby said. "But I do think we need to talk to the mayor. We should ask him to come in here and discuss things with us. It might make us feel better."

"Do you think Brett has informed him of Pam's death?" Maggie asked.

"He probably told the mayor before he told us," she said. "He's probably trying to figure out what to do himself."

"I'm going to text Dana and invite them both to come in here and speak with us," Maggie repeated. She pulled her phone out of her pocket and fired off a quick text. "She said they'll be at the back door in five minutes."

"I'm going to grab those stools out of the store room so we can all chat back here," Ruby said.

"I'm going to run and start a fresh pot of coffee up front," Maggie said. "I have a feeling we might need it."

Maggie swiftly moved to the front. She watched the crowd out the windows while the coffee brewed. She was glad to see the people gathered at the other end of the parking lot in front of Flo's food truck. Myra and Orson appeared busy as well. The crowd there was at least eight people deep.

She hated to think of canceling the festival, but a woman had been murdered. Her heart ached for the older woman who had just been there. Her thoughts were interrupted by a noise in the back. She heard Ruby call out to let her know Dana and the mayor were there. She headed back through the swinging door just as Ruby let them inside.

"I've just started a fresh pot of coffee," Maggie announced. "It should be ready in a few minutes."

"Excellent," Mayor Savino said. Ruby motioned to the stools around the baker's table.

"Please, let's have a discussion before any more time passes," Maggie said. She took a seat at the end of the table.

"We are so sorry to hear about Pam Carter's death," Ruby said. "She was just here, and she was so excited about the festival."

The mayor nodded his head. "She was excited to promote the town of Dogwood Mountain in any way she could."

"What do you think we ought to do?" Ruby said. "Forgive me for getting right to the point."

"No, that's just what we need to do," Mayor Savino said. "I have spoken to the police chief and don't think he is convinced that her death has anything to do with the festival."

"If it turns out that it does, I think we should absolutely cancel," Dana said. "There is no reason to put the public in danger."

"I don't think any of us dispute that," the mayor said. He rubbed his forehead with the palm of his hand. Maggie noted the tinge of gray above his temples. She wondered how old he was and whether the stress of the situation was bad for him.

"I think the coffee is ready," Maggie announced. She rushed through the door and placed four ceramic mugs on a tray along with assorted sweeteners and creamers. She poured the coffee into a carafe and headed back to the kitchen.

"That looks great, Maggie, thank you," Mayor Savino said. He helped himself to a cup.

"There is another complication that I think we ought to share with you," Ruby said. "Pam came here to try a few samples of what we were going to be offering this weekend. When she was here, a truck came racing into the parking lot, revving its engine. Just after that, she ran out of here and no one had seen or heard from her until, well... you know."

"That sounds like every young man in the county on a Saturday night, including my own son," Mayor Savino laughed. "I don't think the police have determined that the truck had anything to do with her death. As I heard it, the truck went the other way."

"Really? I heard she went after it," Dana added before she prepared her coffee.

Maggie looked between them. "Okay, but the same truck appeared this morning as we were walking to work from my house," Maggie said. "He was aggressive when he drove past us. We had to hide between a couple of trees to get out of the way."

"It was like something out of a Stephen King novel," Ruby said.

"Chief Mission assured me that he will increase patrols around the festival over the weekend," the mayor said. "I have no doubt the blue truck is just some troublemaker joyriding around town."

"I don't know, Mayor," Dana said. Her face paled slightly when she glanced at Maggie. "We hope the driver of the truck isn't targeting anyone specific."

"You're not the only one," Maggie said.

The mayor nodded and sipped his coffee. Maggie heard a slight tap on the back door. "I wonder who that is?" Ruby said and rose to open it.

"Is the mayor still in here?" Brett asked as soon as she opened it.

"In here, Chief," the mayor said. "We're just having some coffee and trying to figure out if we should shut things down or not this morning."

Brett walked into the store room and returned with a stool for himself. "I hope you don't shut it down," he said.

"Why's that?" Dana sipped her coffee and leaned in toward him. Maggie felt a slight chill when Dana tossed her hair back over her shoulder. She focused a little too much on Brett for Maggie's liking.

"As we discussed before, we have absolutely no evidence that Ms. Carter's death has anything to do with the spring fling," he said. "But if a lot of people in town are gathered in one place, it makes our job a little easier to keep an eye on things around here."

"Do you think we'll have any trouble?" Dana asked him. She reached her hand toward his arm. Maggie bit the inside of her lip.

Brett shook his head. "I'm not worried about it," he said. "Pam's car wasn't found too close to us. Nothing indicates we have a threat here in town."

"Nothing indicates there isn't, either," Dana pointed out. "On the other hand, I know Pam and her husband had been arguing about when it was time for them to retire. This is just awful."

"I think the festival should go on as planned," Mayor Savino announced, putting finality to the situation. "We'll tell anyone who expresses concern that the police are spending extra time around the festival to make sure everyone remains safe."

"What do we do if this pale blue pickup truck decides to come back around?" Maggie asked. "And what if this time they decide to crash the event, literally?"

"Well, first we have to hope that won't happen. From what we know so far, the driver isn't interested in hurting anyone. If they come around, you call one of us right away," Brett said. "And if you can safely do so, take a picture of the truck with your cell phone and send it right to me."

Everyone agreed to do as Brett said, wanting to follow the law, but it was easy to see that no one felt nearly as comfortable as they made themselves out to be.

CHAPTER NINE

By nine o' clock, the food truck had sold out of the new strawberry fritters for the third time. Maggie returned to the kitchen to mix up another batch. She poured flour into the stand mixer and headed to the cooler for the cream cheese. Myra breezed by her with a new tub of frosting from the store room. "I think we're selling out of a lot of things," she said and set the tub down on the table.

"Yeah, and the midday rush hasn't even started yet," Maggie said.

"I wonder how things are going to sell with our boxed lunches and Flo's food truck?" Myra asked. "It seems like we're each other's competition for lunch."

Maggie set the block of cream cheese on the baker's table and cut through the wrapper. "I don't think we're her competition," she said. "I mean, you're more of an expert on marketing then me, but what we offer is so much different than diner food. Ours is more like tasty cafeteria food for people on the go."

Myra nodded her head and smiled. "You're right. I didn't think of it that way," she said. "It is a very different menu. And speaking of her menu, I can't believe how she has things already organized and ready to go. She's going to really make a go of this."

"I hope so," Maggie said. "I really do after what she has been through."

Myra agreed and picked up the frosting. "I guess I better head back out there," she said.

"Wait, just one question," Maggie said. "Are you ever going to tell us what's going on between you and Orson? Every time someone brings it up, he gets mean, and you get squirrely."

She sighed. "Just a quarrel between roommates is all. I promise we will tone it down and leave our issues at home."

Maggie was skeptical but she wasn't going to beg for answers. "If you say so."

Myra smiled and headed out the door toward the front. Maggie turned her attention back to the batter in the stand mixer. She glanced at the deep fryer on the other side of the kitchen. Maybe she ought to fry up a bunch of the fritters in the big fryer rather than taking the batter out to the food truck. Then they could keep the fritters in the warming drawer and serve them faster.

Instead, she decided to double the batch of batter and fry up a few while she was still in the kitchen but bring the remainder to Myra as planned. The rest she would deliver around to the vendors. She was interested in hearing the scuttlebutt around the festival about the death of the city council member.

Less than an hour later, Maggie hefted a large bucket of fritter batter out to the food truck. "It's more like a batch and a half," she explained to Myra when she put the bucket down. "I have about three dozen fresh fritters in a basket inside. Do you mind hanging out a little while longer so I can walk those around to different vendors? I thought it would be nice to share."

"You'll have to swing back by and tell me all about the gossip you hear," Myra said with a wink. "Oh, and I am sure you will be sending a new horde of customers this way, once they get a whiff of the strawberry and cinnamon in those fritters."

Maggie left her again with a chuckle and a nod. Myra was right. The scent of the fritters would send the crowd running to the food truck. She headed straight for the bookstore tent and smiled at Faylene as she approached.

"Get up and let this lady have a seat," Faylene commanded the young man seated in the upholstered wingback chair that was a twin to her own.

"I brought you some goodies," Maggie announced. She pulled the linen towel back to reveal the hot fritters.

"What a gem," Faylene declared. She helped herself to a fritter. "Oh, these are magical."

Maggie turned to the young man who had vacated his seat for her. "There's one in here for you," she said. The boy smiled and reached for a fritter.

"How's business?" Maggie asked.

"Pretty good," the older woman replied between bites. "You might not expect it, but we've actually done quite well."

"Have you? I've got to admit that I am shocked an event like this would bring many book enthusiasts out," Maggie said. She hesitated. "And I've been worried that the death of Pam Carter would cast a shadow over the weekend."

"I heard about that, but I don't think the death was related to this weekend," Faylene said. "And it happened away from town. I don't know much, but

I've yet to hear anything that would tie it to this weekend."

"I haven't heard anything along those lines, either," Maggie said. "We did have a conversation this morning with the mayor to determine if we should cancel things."

Faylene folded up her napkin and sipped from her water bottle. "I figured as much when I saw the mayor and the city clerk sneak around the back of the donut shop," she said. "When the police chief pulled up, it basically confirmed it."

"Not too easy to keep secrets around here," Maggie said with a smile. "Do you think we should have canceled it?"

"Oh, no," she said and waved her hand in the air. "I have a feeling we will find out in a few weeks that Pam Carter was the unfortunate victim of a random highway robbery. She was found in her car out on a county road. Unfortunately, it's not uncommon these days."

Maggie sighed. She felt a little reassured by Faylene's words. "I suppose we'll find out everything in due time," she said. "I should excuse myself and pass these fritters around before they get too cold."

"Come back and see me when you have more treats to share," Faylene said.

"Is that the only condition by which I am allowed to visit?" Maggie asked. She smiled broadly at her friend.

"Well." Faylene leaned back and appeared to consider the notion. "I suppose you could come around again if you are inclined to talk about books."

Maggie left her with a pat on her shoulder and headed to the next vendor. She passed around the fritters and enjoyed the compliments in return. No one else mentioned Pam Carter's death, or any feeling of concerns over safety. She arrived at Flo's food truck and handed over the last two fritters.

"You may want to warm these up before you eat them," she said.

"I'll take mine as is," Jake announced. He accepted the fritter from Maggie and disappeared inside the truck.

"You like those cold?" she asked him through the window.

"I like them hot or cold or any way in between," Jake said around a full mouth.

"Just how many of those have you had?" Flo asked him.

"I don't know," Jake answered. "Maybe six or seven. Today anyway."

Maggie shared a laugh with Flo. "I guess we both

know who's to blame if we begin to see a decline in profits."

"I want to know where you put it," Maggie called to Jake. She turned back to Flo. "I don't think the boy has a bit of fat on him."

"That's not true," Jake said. Maggie could tell his mouth was full again. "I have to buy new jeans. My old ones are too tight on me now."

Maggie laughed again. "I am not unhappy to hear that," she said. "I suppose I should return to the truck and give Myra a break."

"Before you go," Flo said quietly. "Should we be worried about this councilwoman's death?"

Maggie shook her head. "Brett doesn't think so," she said. "We'll see more of a police presence around than we expected, but aside from that, I don't think we will notice anything."

Flo seemed satisfied with her answer. Maggie carried her empty basket back toward the food truck and wound her way through the crowd gathered in front of the windows.

"Need a hand?" she asked Myra when she climbed up into the truck.

"You could say that," Myra said. "You and your tasty fritters have made this place busier than ever."

CHAPTER TEN

By the time the sun was setting, Maggie was tired beyond her ability to describe. She made a final check over the kitchen preparations for the following morning and set out to find Ruby. After the hazardous walk that morning, they had agreed to ride home together in her pickup truck. Jake had already gone home on foot once for a midday nap and then returned to help Flo late into the night.

"Is there any chance you are ready to go home?" Maggie asked her best friend when she found her walking around outside.

"I was debating on finding you and asking you the same question," Ruby said. "I feel like my feet are going to fall off."

"We still have two more full days left," Maggie said. "Who's crazy idea was this anyway?"

"I seem to remember a conversation you started not too long ago," Ruby said. She draped her arm around Maggie's shoulders and led her toward the donut shop.

"We're heading out for the night," Maggie said to Myra and Brooks when she passed them near the food truck.

"Don't take any offense to this, but you ladies look a bit like death warmed over," Brooks said.

"Oh, no offense taken," Ruby said in an exaggerated tone. "But don't be surprised if you end up with a funny tasting donut the next time you come around."

"Sounds delicious," Brooks said, matching her tone.

Maggie pulled Ruby along to the truck. A minute later, they were in front of her garage. "You'll forgive me if I just let you out and head home, right?" she asked.

"You'll forgive me if I go inside and collapse on my bed, won't you?" Maggie answered.

Ruby laughed and waved at her from the cab of the truck. Maggie counted the steps as she walked to the back door. She pushed the key into the lock and let herself inside. She dropped her bag on the table and ignored the clothes she left in a line behind her. By the time she reached her bedroom, she pulled a pair of pajamas from her drawer, quickly dressed, and fell onto her made bed without turning down the sheets.

She slept hard until the sound of a revving engine roused her from her sleep. She sat upright in bed and reached for her phone which was normally on her nightstand plugged into the charger. But she had left the phone in her bag. She slipped from her bed and padded out into the hall. When she reached the living room she could see the lights flooding the back of her house. The truck was in the backyard.

It was in the back of her house, just feet from her back door.

Jake. If he was home, he would come out of the garage to find out what was going on. She feared what might happen to him if he stepped out into the night. She crouched down on the floor and crawled across the kitchen. When she found her bag she pulled out her phone and prayed that she still had ample battery left.

Seven percent. She sighed and dialed Brett's cell phone number.

"Hello," he answered. His voice was husky.

Immediately she felt bad for calling him instead of 911.

"Brett," she said quietly. "The truck is back. It's in my yard."

"I'll be right there. Can you see the driver?" Brett asked, suddenly very alert.

"He has his high beams on, and they are all I can see out the windows," she said. She waited and held up the phone when the engine roared again. "Did you hear it?"

"I'm on my way," he said. "Text Jake and tell him to stay inside."

Maggie fired off a text as fast as her fingers could move over the screen.

"I called the police," Jake replied. "As soon as I heard the engine I knew it was the truck from this morning."

"Brett knows. Just lay low until he gets here," she wrote. She tucked the phone under her arm and crawled toward the windows on the side of the dining room. The headlights were angled away from the window. She pulled the curtain to the side and carefully pushed herself up enough that she could see the back of the house.

The glow from the outside utility light illuminated the pickup just enough that she could see the pale blue color. She opened her camera app, turned off the flash, and raised the screen to the window. She snapped photos until the battery alerted that it was almost out of life.

She crouched back down under the window and waited. The truck stopped revving the engine and simply idled in the yard, just as it had earlier. She closed her eyes tightly and shook her head. There was no coincidence to explain away the presence of the truck behind her house. The truck racing through her parking lot was not a coincidence.

She shuddered when she thought about the encounter the morning before. Did the driver mean to harm her?

What she wanted to know more than anything else at that moment was whether the driver had been responsible for Pam Carter's death. More than ever, she wondered why the older woman raced out of the donut shop when the truck made its appearance.

Her thoughts were interrupted by the brief wail of a siren. She sat up and looked outside again. Brett was parked behind the pickup, blocking it in the yard. The driver of the truck revved his engine again, several bursts in quick succession. Maggie wondered if he would throw something through the engine block itself.

A second car pulled up, this time angled opposite from Brett's. Maggie could see the Dogwood Mountain Police Department emblem on the side of the car. She wondered if it was Brooks or another officer.

In the glare of the second car's headlights, Maggie could see Brett's car door open. He stepped out with his gun leveled at the pickup.

"Shut down the engine and step out of the vehicle," he shouted over the roar of the engine. "Shut it down now!"

She shivered when he walked around the car door and crossed in front of the other car's lights. The door of the second vehicle opened and the officer stepped out with his gun drawn and trained on the truck.

Brett advanced toward the cab of the truck. Once more the din of the engine died down to an idle. "Shut the engine off," he yelled again. "Shut it down!"

Maggie closed her eyes when he was just feet from the truck. For a moment, she thought the driver would comply and at least some of her questions would be answered. She opened her eyes again. For a few tense moments, Maggie waited while Brett remained outside the truck with his gun drawn and the driver remained inside.

The truck revved again, and the driver threw his truck into reverse. He sped backward and clipped the front of Brett's car, and then sped toward the house. Maggie screamed and covered her head. There was no time to move out of the way. She braced for the truck to crash through the back of her house. In the split second she had to think, she prayed that it would miss her.

But the sound of the engine moved around the side of the house. She jumped to her feet in time to see the taillights as the truck tore through her side yard.

Brett holstered his gun and ran back to his cruiser. In a second he went down the road with the other officer right behind him. Maggie waited for a minute, then pulled the back door open and raced to the garage.

"Jake," she called out. "Jake! Are you okay?"

He opened the door and stepped outside. "Are they gone?"

"Yes, for now," Maggie said.

"I was sure he was going to drive that truck right through the back of your house," Jake said. In the hazy light Maggie could see how pale he had become.

"You and me both," Maggie said.

"Do you think that it is safe to go back inside?"

Maggie nodded. "I'm fairly sure we won't be alone tonight," she said. "If the chief himself doesn't come back here, he will surely send another officer to watch over things."

"I hope they catch him," Jake said before he walked back into the garage and shut the door behind him.

"So do I," Maggie muttered and walked back toward the house.

CHAPTER ELEVEN

Maggie moved to her room and plugged her phone into the charger. As soon as it was plugged in, she heard the notification chime for her text messages. She turned the phone over and read a message from Brett.

"I'm coming back to your house. No argument. Will sleep on the couch."

Maggie set the phone back on her night stand and exhaled. She ran to the bathroom and brushed her teeth. "This is stupid," she said to her reflection. But she ran her fingers through her hair and splashed water on her face. She dried her face off and examined the dark circles under her eyes. "Don't be stupid," she spoke to her reflection again.

Back in her room, Maggie picked up her phone

and texted Jake a quick warning that Brett was coming back. She set the phone down again and moved to her closet for a spare pillow and a couple of blankets for Brett.

Not long after, she saw his headlights in her windows again. He parked his car in the street in front of her house. Maggie ran her fingers through her hair once more and headed to the front door.

"I don't use this door much," she said when she had to pull extra hard to get it open for him.

"I would have parked in the back, but I want Brooks to come out and take photos of the tire tracks in the yard," he said. "I didn't want to drive over it."

"What happened when you chased him?" She moved out of the way and let him inside.

"He had a little bit of a head start on us," Brett said. He moved to the couch and took off his boots.

Maggie set the pillow against the arm rest. "He was also driving very recklessly through town. We backed off a bit and contacted the sheriff's department with a description of the truck."

"I take it they didn't have any better luck catching him?"

Brett shook his head. "Not yet. I don't think anyone was in the immediate area," he said. "But in the morning, some of my officers are going to assist them in a county-wide sweep for the pickup."

"How about you? Are you going out?"

"Nope." He smiled up at her. "I'll be hanging out right here until morning and then sticking around the festival in plain clothes all day. Brooks is going to run our end of the investigation. You'll probably see him and a few others hanging around out of uniform."

"Do you still think we should keep the spring fling going? Is it too risky now?"

"It's still risky, but I think it is even more reason to keep the festival open and the police presence there high," he said.

"High and unnoticed," she said.

"Yes," Brett agreed. "We'll be around all day and into the night."

"Oh, speaking of night." She ran back to her room for her phone. "I got a few pictures of the truck when it was out back. I haven't looked at them to see if they are any good." She handed the phone over to him.

He scrolled through the photos. "I'm going to email some of these to the station," he said. "I'll have dispatch send them out to the county and our officers on patrol. I have the video from my dash camera, but these are the best still photos we have gotten so far."

He handed the phone back to her when he was finished.

Maggie took the phone back and stood awkwardly for a moment. "Are you hungry? Do you want something to drink?" she asked.

Brett shook his head. "I suggest we get some rest while we can," he said. "If you hear anything, I want you to get downstairs to the basement and stay there until I tell you it's clear, okay? I'm going to get a little rest, but if he comes back I will hear him. I also have a night patrol making regular rounds in this neighborhood."

"Okay," Maggie said. "And in the morning?"

"If you don't mind, I'll grab a shower before we leave," he said.

"Before we leave?"

"Oh, yeah, I'm your ride to work. I've texted Ruby and told her to meet us at the donut shop. I don't want her hanging around there without me around," he said.

"Alright," Maggie said. "I'll make sure you're awake in time."

She turned to head back to her bedroom.

"And Maggie," Brett called to her. "I don't want you to worry. I will protect you."

CHAPTER TWELVE

Maggie groaned when she heard her alarm just a few short hours later. She threw her arm over her head and turned back toward the middle of her bed for a moment. Images of the incident from the night before filled her mind and she sat straight up.

"Brett is asleep on my couch," she said and sprang from her covers. She rushed to her closet and picked out an outfit for the workday, then grabbed her underclothes and headed straight for the shower. When she emerged a few moments later, she dressed as fast as she could and toweled off her hair. She felt the pressure to hurry for some reason.

She stood in front of the foggy mirror and wiped the film away with her arm. Her wet hair hung limply over her shoulders. She shrugged and pulled her hair back in a quick French braid, then with her comb pulled a few strands loose from the front.

"No need to look like a middle-aged school marm from a hundred years ago," she said to herself. She added a few swipes of mascara over her lashes and some lip gloss over her lips. She tucked the lip gloss in the pocket of her jeans and headed out of the bathroom, straight for the linen closet.

"Good morning," Brett said when he stepped into the hallway behind her. Maggie felt her cheeks redden a little at the raspy sound of his morning voice.

"Morning," she said and stretched her arms out in front of her. "Towels. Here you go. For your shower."

"Okay," he said and accepted the towels from her. "You don't happen to have any men's shampoo or body wash, do you?"

"Men's body wash?" Her mind raced for a moment. She couldn't remember the last time she felt this awkward.

Brett's face reddened this time. "I'm not implying that you have any regular overnight male guests or anything," he said.

"Oh, no. I don't! I mean, I do," she said. "I do have some men's products, that is. I keep some here for Bradley just in case."

Brett's face relaxed at the mention of her son. "Awesome, thank you, Bradley," he said.

Maggie turned back to the hall closet and retrieved a bottle of body wash and another of shampoo for him. "I hope this works," she said.

"Better than going around smelling like lavender and vanilla all day," he said. "Can you imagine the guff the guys would give me?" He looked up and smiled at her. Maggie stared back at him for a second.

"Lavender and vanilla? You don't like lavender and vanilla?"

"Oh, no, I love it on you," he said. "I mean, that is what you wear, right? I always smell lavender and vanilla in your hair."

They stood there for a long, awkward moment. Maggie was the first to speak. "I'm going to let you get your shower," she said and turned on her heels back to her bedroom.

A few minutes later, Brett was out of the bathroom and pulling on his boots. Maggie noted the new jeans and V-neck sweater. He looked more like an English professor than a police chief.

"We can have coffee when we get to the donut shop," Maggie said. "I'll start a pot as soon as we get there. Oh, and if you want a regular breakfast instead of donuts, I can make something."

"You mean there's more to breakfast than donuts?" Brett teased. "Who knew?"

"That's a better question than I expected for you to ask," Maggie said. She pulled her extra sweatshirt from the coat closet.

"What did you expect me to say?"

"Something like, 'you mean you can actually cook and not just make donuts?'"

Brett laughed. "Oh, give me a little credit. I'm a smarter man than that," he said and headed to the front door. "Is it okay if I leave my bag here for now?" Maggie noticed a black duffel bag for the first time.

"When did you bring that inside?" she asked.

"Last night when I got here. You didn't see it then?"

"No. I never saw it," she said. "And yeah, of course you can leave it here. In fact. You can put it in the guest bedroom if you think you'll be here again tonight. I should have offered last night."

"Are you inviting me to spend the night tonight, Maggie?"

She replied by tossing a throw pillow in his face. "I'll be in the car," she said.

"You might as well wait on me," Brett said. "It's

my car." Maggie rolled her eyes and headed out the front door in front of him.

"I just texted Ruby that we're here," she said a few minutes later when they arrived at the donut shop.

"I'm surprised she isn't here yet," he said. "Did she reply?"

"She just did. She's on her way," Maggie said. She breathed a little sigh of relief. So far the light blue pickup truck had not made an appearance anywhere near her farm, but she wasn't sure that it wouldn't.

Maggie turned the key in the back door and waited while Brett went in ahead of her. She waited just inside the door while he made his way through the entire building.

"All clear," he said when he returned to the kitchen.

"Thanks," Maggie said. She locked the door behind her and headed for her office. After she dropped off her bag and sweatshirt, she pulled off her coat and laid it over the desk. "Do you want to wait back here or out front?"

Brett shrugged. "I'll be all over the place," he said. "But I might hang out back here with you for a little while. I've never seen what you do in the mornings."

"I'm going to get some coffee going," she said and breezed past him through the swinging door.

Once the coffee was brewing, Maggie returned to the back and opened the cooler door. "You never told me what you want for breakfast."

"I thought I would just start with coffee and wait a little while to eat," he said.

Maggie nodded and let the door close behind her. She grabbed the large tub of butter and headed back out into the kitchen. "You're waiting for Ruby to get here, aren't you?" she asked him as soon as she stepped out.

"Waiting for Ruby? What do you mean?" he asked without looking at her.

"Ruby is the chef. I get it," she said. "I may not be as good as she is, but I can hold my own in the kitchen."

"Oh, hush. I know you can. You've cooked for me before, remember?"

Maggie smirked, enjoying giving him a hard time.

Brett cleared his throat and pointed toward the office. "Are your security cameras working? I think I'll monitor things from there for a little while."

Maggie nodded and turned her attention to the

store room. She grabbed a large bag of sugar and another of flour and headed back to the baker's table.

"Ruby is here," Brett announced from the office.

"Thank goodness," Maggie said under her breath. She headed for the door and twisted the lock.

"Thanks," Ruby said when she stepped inside. "I'm sorry I'm a little late."

"Hi, Ruby," Brett called from the office. "Any problems coming in?"

"No problems coming in," she said. "But there is something you're going to need to see."

CHAPTER THIRTEEN

"What do I need to see?" Brett asked when he stepped back into the kitchen. "I hope it's something warm and cheesy."

"He's looking forward to whatever you might make him for breakfast," Maggie said with another smirk.

"I never said that!" Brett said. "She just said she had something for me to look at. Naturally, I hope it's something she made me to eat."

"Are you two finished?" Ruby asked. She sent a warning look to Brett. "This is actually something a little serious."

"Okay. I'm all ears." Brett pulled up a stool and sat down.

Ruby moved to the prep table and set her backpack down. She unzipped the top and pulled a laptop out of the bag. "I was expecting an email from my publisher and hadn't seen anything yet," she said. "Once in a while, an email from her office winds up in my spam folder. If a junior editor emails me from their account, it can wind up there."

"Okay," Maggie said. She stepped closer to the sink. "I'm not sure I follow."

Ruby opened the laptop lid. She moved her finger around on the trackpad and opened up her email account. "This is why I ran a little late this morning. I checked the spam folder for a message, and I found this." She pointed to the screen and stepped aside so Maggie could read the email.

"It's from Pam Carter's office," Maggie said.

Brett stood and moved behind Maggie. He read over her shoulder. "She emailed you to ask for you to stop supporting the spring fling. Why? I don't understand."

"Keep reading," Ruby directed.

"'Dear Ms. Cobb,'" Maggie began. "'I am writing to explain my displeasure in the planning of this new spring fling. Despite my earlier support, I have arrived at the opinion that the festival would be an abysmal failure. I also think it is an unfair burden on the taxpayers and people of Dogwood Mountain. I don't want to make a public announcement that might cast a shadow on Dogwood Donuts, so I am asking you privately to abandon your plans. If you do not, I will be forced to publicly denounce the event and pressure Mayor Jason Savino to cancel it outright.'"

"And it was signed by Pamela Carter, "Ruby said.

"I don't understand this. She was just here and never once acted like she wanted to cancel anything," Maggie said.

"Check your spam folder, Maggie," Brett said. "I want to see if you got the same email."

Maggie said nothing but rushed to her office. She moved her coat off of her desk and opened her work computer. "It was in my spam folder, too," she announced as soon as she opened her email account.

"What is the date on the email?" Brett asked.

"Two weeks ago," Maggie answered. "I never saw this."

"Same here. Sent two weeks ago," Ruby said. "But she never told me anything, either. She seemed so excited."

"How soon will Myra be here?" Brett asked. "I want to have her check her spam folder, too."

"I told her to sleep in a bit this morning because she was here so late last night. She has a work email account on my laptop," Maggie said. "She's used it to communicate with vendors here and there."

"And she usually leaves it open," Ruby added. "I don't think it's a violation of her privacy to take a look."

"Why don't you look, Maggie?" Brett said. "Since it's on your computer. If this turns into something, I don't want someone accusing me of stepping outside of their rights."

"I'll look," Maggie said. She closed her own account and opened Myra's up. "There are two emails from Pam Carter's account." She turned her laptop around for Brett and Ruby to see.

"Click on them and see what they say," Brett directed.

"The first one is identical to what we got," Maggie said. "Of course, it is addressed to 'Ms. Sawyer' instead of 'Ms. Sharpe' or 'Ms. Cobb.'"

"What about the other one?" Ruby asked.

Maggie turned the computer back and clicked on the second message. "Uh, we might have a problem," she said and scanned through the email. "You need to read this, Brett."

He stepped around behind her chair and rested his hand on her shoulder as he read. "'I tried to be nice about this, Ms. Sawyer. But since you are still advertising this event, I am going to have to go to the mayor. And I will tell him how you've been in trouble with the law in the past. If you don't want this or any other bad things to happen to you, stop it right now. Announce it in the paper that the festival is canceled.'"

"None of this makes any sense," Ruby said. "Why would Pam Carter email any of us to cancel the spring fling? She has been so supportive from the start of this whole thing! I spoke to her personally before we applied for the permits for it."

"I'll be right back," Brett said, walking out to the kitchen. Maggie heard him speaking on the phone with someone. "Another officer will be here in a moment. I have to step out for a little while."

"Where are you going?"

"I need to run to my office and fill out some paperwork as fast as I can," he said. He headed for the back door. Maggie followed him to lock it back up tight.

"When will the other officer be here?" she asked. It was just after five in the morning.

"He should be coming down the alley right about now," Brett said. He pulled the door open. A large yellow envelope fell inside when he opened it.

"What's that?"

"Don't touch it," Brett said. "Can you hand me a pair of those disposable gloves?" Ruby grabbed a pair and handed them to Brett, who promptly slipped them on his hands and picked up the envelope.

Maggie watched him turn the envelope over. "There's no writing on the outside of it."

Brett slowly pulled the flap open and looked inside. "It's just some paper. A letter," he said and pulled out a single sheet. "Great."

"What is it? Another letter from Pam?" Maggie asked. She meant no disrespect to the recently deceased woman, but her impatience and exhaustion were getting the best of her.

"There is a cut and paste note that says you should have put the festival to an end and now you are going to be sorry," Brett said. "It doesn't say how you'll be sorry, but it says you were warned."

"It looks like something someone put together during arts and crafts class at preschool," Ruby said. "What are we supposed to do with this?"

"Nothing," Brett said. "This comes with me to the police station for processing as evidence. You stay right here and get ready for the day like normal. Officer Masters is here now, and he can check out your security cameras to see if he can spot anything." He moved out of the way of the officer.

"You should send someone by to check on Orson and Myra," Maggie suggested.

"Brooks has been there all night," Brett said. "Now, I am going to head to the office and get started on a search warrant for Pam Carter's city council computer."

CHAPTER FOURTEEN

Maggie offered the police officer a cup of coffee, which he readily accepted before he went into her office. He made his rounds through the building and outside of the donut shop. When Jake arrived, he escorted him inside. "Why is there a police officer here?" Jake asked as got his apron on.

"Because of last night," Maggie explained. "And because of a threatening note someone left outside the back door."

"After we were already here," Ruby added.

"What in the heck is going on?" Jake asked. He began moving buckets of dough and batter to the dining room for Maggie who announced she was headed out to open the food truck for the day. She nodded to Ruby and Officer Masters who remained behind in the kitchen.

"I don't know what's going on," Maggie said to Jake when they were in the dining room. "After the truck showed up at the house last night, I'm convinced someone has it out for me or maybe all of us." She explained about the emails the three of them had received.

"It would help if we knew who the heck was in that pickup," Jake said.

"I agree with you there," Maggie said. She headed out the front door in front of him. She stepped outside and looked up in the early morning sky. The sun would not be up for a little while yet. Most mornings, Maggie loved the hush of the early hours before dawn. But the air this morning felt colder and sharper than it had just a week before. "I should have brought my coat."

Jake stepped up into the food truck and set the first load on the small counter. "You go ahead and get things turned on out here and I will run back to your office and grab your sweatshirt," he said.

"Thank you," Maggie said. "That's nice of you."

"Miss Florence is teaching me to be a little more conscientious," he said and headed back inside.

Maggie shook her head and chuckled. She hadn't

considered Jake lacking in conscientiousness, but the lessons were clearly making an impact on the young man. She turned her attention to the thermostat and then switched on the mini donut machine and the deep fryer.

"I hope it warms up soon," she said to the empty truck. She placed the dough in the fridge and then ducked into the small bathroom before Jake returned. She chided herself for not going before she came out to the truck, but she had more important things on her mind.

While she was seated, she heard the sudden roar of a familiar engine just outside. "Oh, no," she shouted in fear. The pickup truck was back, and she was outside in the food truck alone without her cell phone.

Maggie jumped to her feet and pulled up and refastened her jeans as quickly as she could. She skipped the sink and pumped hand sanitizer on her hands. The truck engine rumbled just on the other side of the wall of the food truck. Her heart beat wildly. She pulled the bathroom door open slowly. Bright headlights from the pickup glowed outside the door. She was blinded by the brightness.

"Please don't let Jake come running back outside," Maggie begged. She sank to the floor and crawled out into the main area of the truck. She could hear the idle of the truck just feet away. She moved toward the other side and reached her hand into the drawer under the counter and felt around until she felt the cold metal of a knife blade. She pulled the knife out of the drawer and crouched beneath the small table near the back door.

"Please, please just let him go away." For a long moment she sat there and listened to the truck and waited. She could hear the oil heating up in the deep fryer. "Maybe I should just go out there and confront him," she said to herself. She might at least get a good look at the driver. That might be more to go on than they had so far. She moved to her knees and then rose up slightly on her feet. She gripped the knife in her right hand and took in a deep breath.

The driver of the pickup pushed down hard on the accelerator once again. Maggie jumped from the truck's sudden roar and fell backward against the wall. The headlights moved then, and the scream of the engine seemed to be further away. Maggie moved to her feet again and looked outside the truck windows.

The truck had moved to the center of the parking lot. She watched as the driver whipped the truck in a half-circle, narrowly missing the ice cream vendor's tent. A police car had moved around the side of the building, blocking the exit to the road. The truck moved forward again suddenly and stopped just short of ramming into the police cruiser. Another pair of headlights appeared and pulled into the parking lot, followed by a third car. She recognized Brett's Iroc Z24. She was quite sure the second police car belonged to Brooks.

All three vehicles surrounded the pickup. Maggie watched as Officer Masters walked over to him with his gun raised. Brett was parked the closest to the passenger side of the truck. She watched as he opened his car door and moved to the truck. Maggie could see the outline of the driver's head. His attention appeared to be on Officer Masters' gun.

In a flash, Brett was inside of the cab with his gun just inches from the driver. A second later, the truck shut down and the driver had been pulled outside by Officer Masters. He was against the side of the truck with the large police officer pinned against him.

Maggie dropped the knife on the floor and went out the back door of the food truck. She headed straight for the driver. Officer Masters had pulled the man's arms behind him and placed his wrists in handcuffs.

The man was dressed in faded blue jeans and a tan

colored sweatshirt. She raised her finger and stopped about a foot from the stranger.

"Who are you?" she shouted at the top of her lungs. "Why are you harassing me? Why were you at my house in the middle of the night?"

"Maggie, Maggie," Brett said softly. She felt gentle pressure on her arms as he pulled her back. "Step back and let us do our jobs."

"No! I want to know who this man is and why he is threatening my life!"

The man raised his eyes to her. His face was covered in dirt and old acne scars. Despite his bulky body, his face was thin. She could see the outline of his cheekbones. He looked at her with his glazed and vacant eyes.

"You Maggie?" he asked.

"Why were you doing this to me if you don't even know who I am?" she asked again. Her voice was low and threatening.

The man dropped his head. Tufts of unwashed gray hair poked out all over the back of his head. "It ain't meant to threaten your life. Just to scare you a little," he said at last. His voice was deep and raspy.

"What do you have against me?" she asked a little more softly.

"I don't got anything against you," the old man

said. He raised his eyes again. "I was just doing a job. That's all. Somebody paid me to come around and scare you a little. I wouldn't never hurt a lady."

"Who hired you?" Brooks asked behind her. "Can you tell us who paid you?"

The old man shook his head. "I don't know who it was. I just know I found a note in my mailbox asking me to drive all the way up here and give you a scare," he said. "Wasn't a name on the note. Said they would pay me five hundred dollars to come up here and drive around your place and give you a scare."

"Where are you from?" Officer Masters asked. "You said they paid you to drive up here."

"I live down in Flippin on the other side of the line," he said.

"What's your name?" Brett asked at last.

He dropped his head again. "I'd rather not say."

"You better say," Brett said. His voice was tight. "And you better start giving me a better story than this.

Right now, you're in a lot of trouble. But if you don't start making a believer out of me, you might just find yourself charged with the murder of Pam Carter."

"Murder?" The man's head whipped up again. "I ain't killed nobody. I just drove around and scared her, about a month ago. That's how I know the note writer was good for the money. They already paid me once after I ran around the old lady's house a few times. Left the money right there in my mailbox at the end of the gravel driveway."

"For the last time, what is your name?"

"Perkins," he said slowly. "Cletus Perkins."

"Do you have any family up here, Cletus?" Brett asked.

"Yes, sir," the old man said. "My great-niece Dana lives up here. She has a real good job with the city, too. She can vouch for me. She'll tell you I ain't no murderer."

CHAPTER FIFTEEN

An hour later, the truck was gone, and the lot was filled with vendors and festival attendees.

Maggie sat at the table in the food truck sipping a cup of coffee. Orson hovered over her. "You need to go straight home," he said.

"We have a business to run," Maggie countered. "And this is the busiest weekend we've had since this summer. I have to be here."

"You have to go home and rest after what you've been through," Orson said again.

"Well, I'll be at the police station at noon," she said. "I have to give my statement. Cletus Perkins is going to be arraigned first thing Monday morning."

"They ought to let him out for a few hours," Orson mumbled. "Let me get my hands on him. Then they won't have to worry about an arraignment on Monday."

"Orson, they need to find out if Cletus Perkins killed Pam Carter," she said. "Because if he didn't do it, there is a murderer around here somewhere."

"Why don't you run back inside the donut shop and bring me some more ground coffee?" Orson asked. "I'm running low."

Maggie glanced at the full bag she had brought in the day before when she closed up for the night. She dropped her head and sighed. "Okay, Orson. I'll run after the coffee for you." She left the food truck and walked across the sidewalk to the front door of the donut shop. The air outside had warmed a little, but she still felt a cold chill on her skin.

"Are you taking another break?" Ruby asked when she entered the kitchen. "You were just in here forty-five minutes ago."

"I'm aware," Maggie said and slumped onto a stool. "I have lost all control out there. Orson acts like I am no longer capable of running my own business."

"What did he send you after this time?"

"More coffee," Maggie said. "There is a five pound sack sitting right there in the open."

"He's capable of running circles around us sometimes," Ruby said. "You could just hang out here with me for an hour. By then it will be time to leave and go to the police station."

"But what will Orson do without ten pounds of coffee?" she asked. She shook her head and laughed.

"We'll see how long he lasts," Ruby said. She packed fresh apples into the boxed lunches and set them into the box. "Jake promised to come after these at eleven. Until then, I'm going to sit."

"I can't believe it's the middle of the morning and we're just going to sit around for a little while," Maggie said.

"You really ought to heed Orson's words," Ruby said. "What you have been through the last few days has been awful."

"I don't disagree with that," she said. "It's just that the longer I sit, the more I think about it and the worse I feel."

"Come and sit anyway and talk to me about it," Ruby said. She gently guided Maggie out of the kitchen and into the dining room. "With the lights over the counter off we should be able to sit down in peace for a little while."

Maggie simply nodded and made her way to the booth on the far side of the counter. She eased herself into the seat and rested her elbows on the table. "Sitting in peace sounds good right now," she said. "I would like to do a little more of that."

"How about outside under the stars in your favorite wooden chair?" Ruby said. "When all of this is over, we will sit around a roaring fire again and feel the cool night air and sit in peace."

Maggie sighed deeply. "Sounds good to me."

"You must have been terrified this morning in the food truck," Ruby said. "It was smart to duck down low and hide when you saw the truck."

Maggie pressed her lips together. "I didn't see it," she said. "I heard it. I was in the bathroom."

Ruby covered her mouth with her hand. "You were in the bathroom when he showed up and started revving up that stupid truck? Oh, you poor thing," she said. She reached for Maggie's hand. "We need to talk this out."

"Why? We've both been through things before," she said. "This one isn't any different."

"Yes, it is," Ruby said. "You need to talk about it here before you make your statement down at the police station."

Maggie nodded. "I know you're right," she said. "I just don't think everything has hit me quite yet. I'm tired, you know? It feels like winter came overnight and took up residence in my bones. I can't get warm."

"You definitely need a break. Why don't you just head home after you make your statement?" Ruby suggested.

"Because this is my business and I need to work. I'll be right back," she said. "I want to read those emails again." She headed for the back to get her laptop.

"I'll get us a snack," Ruby said.

"Ummm, I think I know what Orson's problem is and you're never going to believe it," Maggie said when she returned.

"Please tell me he didn't break up with Gretchen." Ruby frowned as she sat back down. "Oh, wait. His issue is with Myra this time, isn't it?"

"I know it's hard to keep up, but this is serious. I feel like I've invaded her privacy now but look at this." Maggie turned the laptop screen to face her friend.

"Engaged? Myra is engaged?" Ruby gasped as she read the email from a local Justice of the Peace.

"And she didn't tell us!" Maggie said slowly. "I bet Orson found out and is upset because that means she'll be moving out."

"Somehow..." Ruby sighed. "I'm simultaneously thrilled for Brooks and Myra and feeling terrible for Orson."

"Terrible for Orson about what?" he bellowed. "About how I never got the coffee I asked for, because I think that's pretty terrible too."

Maggie and Ruby's eyes both shot in his direction, both unable to form a sentence.

"Earth to the crazy people. What's wrong with you all now?"

"Oh, Orson," Maggie said. "We accidentally just came across an email of Myra's…"

Orson huffed and interrupted her. "And now you know that she's not only getting hitched, but she's moving out and leaving me all alone. She didn't even bother to ask me to be an usher or anything. You know, just because I'm old, doesn't mean I can't participate in things."

"Hold on just a second," Ruby cut in. "You should be happy for her. Yes, it's a little sad that she will be moving out, but it's not like they plan on getting married tomorrow or anything."

"That's what you think," Orson muttered. "She has it all planned out already. She's going to be upset you all found out before she had a chance to tell you but with this busy weekend and all this mess with the truck, she wanted to wait for the right time. Not that there's ever a right time to do away with old friends."

"Enough! I know you're upset, but no wonder

why you two are fighting. Myra loves you and wants you to be excited for her. Instead, you're crabbing about everything and giving everyone a hard time. Who knows, maybe you'll prefer living alone."

"Or maybe you two can find me another stray." Orson slammed his hands on the table and stormed out of the donut shop.

CHAPTER SIXTEEN

Maggie and Ruby had decided not to let Myra know what they found. If she had plans to tell them in a certain way or at a certain time, then neither wanted to ruin that. When she arrived around eleven, she relieved Orson in the food truck and everyone would just have to hope that he didn't open up his mouth and say anything. Jake stuck around to help her out during the late morning rush, which occurred later than normal during the festival.

"I'm going to drive you," Brooks appeared and announced. "To the station, I mean."

"No, that isn't necessary," Maggie said. "I can drive myself."

"Your car is still back at your house," Ruby

pointed out. "I don't think you have time to walk back there and get it. Stop being stubborn."

"Fine." Maggie sighed. She followed Brooks out the front door and into his car. They arrived at the police station a few minutes later.

"You ready?" Brooks asked her before he opened his door. "You know this will be over in like an hour, right? You just have to go in and give your version of the things that happened."

"I know," she said with a smile. "I'm just tired. This guy has interrupted my sleep and peace a lot over the past few days, you know."

"More like terrorized your sleep and your peace," Brooks said.

"Something like that," Maggie said. "But the most important thing here is still to figure out what this man had to do with Pam Carter's death. Yeah, the last few days haven't been fun for me, but I'm still alive and kicking. But it's not just about me. A woman is dead."

"Exactly right," Brooks said. He stepped out of the car and moved to the passenger side. "Let's go get this over with."

"Thanks," Maggie said when he opened her car door.

She walked behind him through the police station

and back to a small, windowless office. "Just have a seat here and Donna will be with you in a second." Maggie smiled. She liked Donna Cooper, a former officer who served as some sort of executive secretary for the entire department.

"Would you like a cup of coffee?" Donna asked her from the hallway just a few minutes later.

"No, thanks," Maggie said. "I have more than enough caffeine in my system already today."

"I bet you do," Donna said. She eased into the chair across a small table from where Maggie was seated. She set her own coffee mug down in front of her. "I guess owning a donut shop would make coffee consumption a daily requirement."

Maggie laughed and nodded her head. "You don't know half of it," she said. "I never knew how much coffee I could consume in a single day until Aunt Marjorie left the place to me."

Donna smiled. She moved her coffee mug to the side and opened the three-ring binder notebook in front of her. "Your aunt was quite the lady," she said. "I sure miss her. And I am sure you do as well."

Maggie nodded her head. "Especially on days like these," she said.

Donna folded her arms over her chest and leaned over the notebook. "All we're going to do here today is get your side of what has been going on," she said. "You've done this before, and this time is no different. Just start talking about the first time you saw the pickup truck and tell me what happened."

Maggie felt slightly better. When she began speaking, the words tumbled out. Donna listened intently and asked only a few questions. After about twenty minutes, she closed the notebook and smiled. "We're done here," she said. "That's all there is to it."

"So, I can go?"

Donna nodded. "Chief Mission told me to send you his way before you go," she said. "Do you remember how to get to his office?"

Maggie nodded and headed down the narrow hall. She was grateful it was Donna she spoke with. At least she didn't have to repeat the same things over and over again.

The door was closed when she reached Brett's office. She waited for a second to listen for voices, then knocked lightly.

"Come on in," Brett called from the other side. He smiled when Maggie opened the door. "How did things go?"

Maggie shrugged. "You know Donna," she said. "She makes it seem like having coffee with a good friend."

"That's why we love her around here," Brett said. He pointed to the chair across from his desk and invited her to sit down.

"I wanted to let you know that the prosecutor offered Cletus Perkins a plea deal," he said.

"Already?" Maggie was taken aback by the news. "That was fast."

"It was fast," Brett said. "I guess the old man realized he was going to jail for a while and decided that he remembered more than he first told us." He sighed and sat forward in his chair. "You should also know that we have made a second arrest. This time, for the murder of Pam Carter."

"You did? How? I mean, who?" Maggie stammered. "What happened in the last few hours?"

Brett lightly placed his palms on the top of his desk. "Brooks drove you here, right?" Maggie nodded in reply. "Would you like to go for a drive with me? I'll fill you in on everything, and we can get you back home where you can pick up your own car."

"Yeah, that's a good idea," Maggie said. She had already forgotten that she was without her own vehicle. Without another word, Brett stood and grabbed his phone off of his desk.

"I'm headed out with Ms. Sharpe," he said to his secretary as he passed by her desk.

Maggie smiled when she saw the Iroc Z24 parked in the chief's parking space in the back of the police station. She loved the car and was glad it wasn't another police car for once.

"Okay to just take you home?" Brett asked.

"Sure," Maggie said. "Now are you going to tell me what has been going on?"

Brett nodded and pulled out onto the road. "Remember when I told you I needed a search warrant?"

"To search Pam Carter's city council office and computer, right?"

"That's how it started," Brett said. "After we picked up Cletus, the prosecutor decided to ask for a broader warrant."

"Search warrant for what?"

"For the entire city hall," Brett said. "And about that time, Mr. Perkins decided to share some more information about his great-niece."

"Dana? Dana Perkins?" Maggie's mind raced. Brett turned onto her street and slowed to a stop in front of her house. Suddenly, the pieces fell together in her mind. "I just watched a movie about this. She used a fake email address, didn't she? But how did she make it look like Pam had sent the emails?"

Brett smiled. "Very good, madam detective," he

said. "Exactly. Dana Perkins faked the emails with a false email account. Apparently there is a way to use a fake account and mask the email address with another one. Thankfully the prosecutor's office is more tech savvy than I am."

"Okay, so she sent the emails and put her great-uncle up to terrorizing me in the hopes that, what, we would stop the festival?"

Brett nodded again. He opened his car door and stepped out. "Let's get inside and I'll tell you about the rest."

Maggie followed him up the walk and opened the front door. "I don't understand why, though," she said.

"What was the point of trying to stop the festival? She never once acted like she didn't want it to go on."

"That's the rest of the story," Brett said. "When we questioned Dana, she swore she never set out to kill Pam Carter. She only wanted to force her to stop the festival. Pam was the head of the tourism committee for the city council. She had sent Cletus up here a month beforehand to harass Pam, only Pam never knew why he did it. Dana didn't convey that message very well."

"Why didn't Pam report it?"

"She did, only she reported it to the county and

not the police department because when she saw him it was outside of the city limits," Brett said.

"Okay, so Dana followed Pam and killed her," Maggie said. "But I still don't get why."

Brett took a seat on the couch where he had spent the night before. "She knew when Cletus showed up in the parking lot it would drive Pam to leave," he said. "Dana was waiting for her, followed her, and acted like a friend merely offering assistance. Only she pulled out a .38 revolver and told her to cancel the spring fling. She swears she never meant to pull the trigger. It was an accident, a byproduct of her desperation."

"Why was she desperate?" Maggie asked as she sat down on the stuffed chair across from the couch. "What would drive her to murder, and what does it have to do with what we had planned?"

"The festival was unexpected, and the mayor decided to use money in the reserve fund to cover the city's expenses. Advertising, extra police presence, even their little booth at the festival," Brett explained.

"Tell me she wasn't embezzling money from the town…" Maggie's eyes were wide.

"Spot on, Sleuth. When she found out about the spring fling, she became nervous because she had already embezzled all the money. She thought she was safe to move things around as she saw fit since the city would be getting the next half of their budget in the coming months."

The picture was becoming clearer. "So, until the spring fling came up, she had what she believed to be a perfect plan to replace the money from the general fund and cover her tracks? Then over the next however long, she could keep moving things around until she felt like she'd properly covered her tracks."

"Yes." Brett nodded. "Before the big audit that she knew was coming. The one that she knew would cause her to lose her job if anyone found out about what she did."

"There's just one problem," Maggie said, sitting up straighter. "If Dana embezzled the money, how did we get approval from the city?"

Brett grinned. "Let's just say you have some good friends in Dogwood Mountain." He stood as though he was preparing to leave.

"I don't think so, Mister." She grabbed at his arm. "Are you saying that someone paid for us to have the spring fling?

"Well, it was obvious the town didn't have the funds they thought they did, but everyone had already agreed, and you all were making so many plans and no one wanted to put a stop to the festival since it truly was a great idea for Dogwood Mountain."

"That was nice of the council, but it still doesn't answer my question," Maggie pointed out, trying not to jump out of her seat with anticipation.

"There was a random anonymous donation," Brett explained.

"And do you just happen to know who that anonymous person is?"

"I couldn't say."

"Okay, well then let me think about this for a moment." Maggie stood and went into the kitchen. She came back with a bag of chips and sat back down. "What? I think better when I'm eating. It helps me concentrate."

Brett stared at her blankly as she ate and mumbled to herself.

"Was it you?" she asked.

"It wasn't." He chuckled and shook his head.

She narrowed her eyes at him and shoved a handful of chip crumbs into her mouth. "Gretchen!" she exclaimed. "Was it Gretchen?" Maggie wiped her mouth and brushed the remaining crumbs off her lap. "She's best friends with Mayor Savino's wife, isn't she? I bet he told his wife and she told Gretchen."

Brett laughed.

"What, more crumbs?" She wiped her mouth again.

"No. It's just that you're right. All it took you was sixty seconds and a half a bag of chips, and you figured it out."

"Brett Mission." Maggie scowled. "I did not eat a half a bag of chips in sixty seconds."

CHAPTER SEVENTEEN

Ruby insisted that Maggie sleep in the next morning, the last day of the spring fling. She decided to listen for once and rose from her bed sometime after nine. She took her time in the shower and dressed in a loose blouse and a pair of jeans. She pulled on her boots and headed for work at ten.

When she pulled into the alley behind the donut shop she was delighted to catch a glimpse of the large crowd in the parking lot. For the last day of the festival, the place was hopping with activity. At eleven, the vendors would count their votes and decide on the best of the festival. And there was no way she was going to miss that.

She could hear the din of voices when she pushed the back door open. Ruby stood in front of the prep table while Jake, Myra, Orson, and Brooks milled around in the center of the kitchen.

"I thought you were going to sleep in," Ruby said to her.

Maggie didn't answer immediately. She looked from one person to the next and raised her hands above her head. "Who is watching the truck?" she asked. "Everyone is here!"

"Go see for yourself," Orson said. He shook his head, but by the smirk on his face she knew the gruffness was put on.

"Go see for myself? I can see for myself. Everyone who is employed by this donut shop is standing in this kitchen," she said, then glanced at Brooks. "Plus one, that is."

"Just go look," Ruby said. Maggie dismissed her growing frustration and headed through the swinging door and out toward the front. She could see a line of people formed in front of the food truck. She pushed open the door and peered inside.

She could hear the sounds of someone bustling around inside the truck, but there was no one visible from the windows. Maggie shrugged and opened the door in the back.

"Brett," she said, startled, when she stepped

inside. He stood over three baskets of mini donuts with the cinnamon and sugar shaker.

Maggie stifled a giggle when he looked up at her. The lines on his forehead and the look in his eyes spoke of an extreme level of panic. He was red faced and sweaty. The front of the apron he had tied over his clothes was smeared with stripes of chocolate and pink frosting.

"Maggie," he said. "I'm trying to keep up. I think I've almost got it."

"Is that coffee almost ready?" a woman's voice called from outside the order window.

"Coming right up!" Brett called out lightly. "As soon as I remember what she ordered."

Maggie brushed past him and opened the second order window. "If you're waiting on something, go ahead and line up here," she said. "Now, what was your coffee order?" The older woman rolled her eyes and repeated her order. Maggie turned to the refrigerator and pulled out the heavy cream and started the cappuccino for the woman.

"I'm waiting on a black coffee and three strawberry fritters," the man beside her said.

"I'll have that to you in just a second," Maggie announced and smiled. She poured the coffee and opened a take-out box and filled it with three fritters.

She handed the coffee to the man and turned back to the milk frother. A few seconds later, she secured the lid on another cup and handed the cup out the window to the older woman.

Brett bagged up the mini donuts and handed them through the window. He glanced again at Maggie, then took the next person's order. Maggie listened, and then turned to fill it as fast as she could.

For fifteen straight minutes, they worked side by side. Brett took the orders while she fulfilled them. Once in a while she caught a glance from him while she breezed around the small kitchen.

When the crowd died down at last, Brett leaned against the counter and wiped the sweat from his face with a napkin.

"I don't know how you do it," he said.

"Why are you doing it?" Maggie asked at last. "There are four people inside that could be out here doing their jobs."

"He insisted," Ruby said behind her. Maggie turned around to see her best friend standing in the doorway. "He was determined to learn how to help out today."

"But why?" Maggie turned back to Brett. "Are you looking for a part-time job?"

"Everyone! Please, everyone, may I have your

attention," Mayor Jason Savino called out from the middle of the parking lot. "Ladies and gentlemen, we would like to have your attention, please."

Ruby stepped back out of the truck. Jake appeared in the doorway instead and stepped up inside. "You might as well let Jake take over, Maggie," Ruby said. "I think Mayor Savino is going to want to hear from the two of us."

"I got it from here, Chief Mission," Jake announced.

"No, I'll stay and help," Brett said.

"Really, it's okay," Jake said. He moved in front of the order window and began taking the next order.

"I think I've been fired," Brett said and untied his soiled apron. He followed Maggie out of the truck and over to where Ruby stood. Myra, Brooks, and Orson joined them.

Mayor Savino ran through a few comments, and then handed out plaques and trophies to various vendors. Ruby accepted the trophy for "Best Coffee in Town" for the donut shop.

"Many of you know that we lost a beloved member of our community and city council this week," Mayor Savino said after the prizes were handed out. "Pam Carter will be missed in this community. She didn't deserve what happened to her.

Beyond that, I cannot say anymore due to the ongoing criminal investigation. Instead, let's hear from Maggie Sharpe and her crew at Dogwood Donuts. The spring fling is the product of their vision for this community."

The mayor offered the portable microphone to Maggie. Ruby gently pushed her forward, and Maggie reluctantly accepted it.

"I want to thank each one of our vendors for their support and participation," Maggie began. "I'm especially proud of my crew. Myra Sawyer took on this project and ran with it." She waited while the crowd applauded. "I hope the past three days have given us the opportunity to showcase the best Dogwood Mountain has to offer. And I sincerely hope this is only the first of many annual spring flings."

Her words were met with more applause and a few cheers from the crowd. "But I propose that we do things a little bit differently next year," she continued.

"Yeah, add more spaces and more parking," someone shouted out.

Maggie nodded her head and chuckled. "I think that's the second priority on my list," she said. "The first is, well, really a proposal. It will be up to the city to decide. But I want to suggest that we change the name to the 'Pam Carter Memorial Spring Fling.'"

For a moment, the crowd was silent. After a moment, the applause began again and swelled for a solid minute.

"I think that's something we can make happen," Mayor Savino said over the rousing applause.

They spent the next hour shaking hands and posing for photos for the local newspaper. Maggie watched as Flo handed out newly printed copies of her menu. She was pleased to hear the number of comments from people who expressed their approval to the news that The Diner food truck would remain in Dogwood Mountain after the festival.

Out of the corner of her eye, Maggie saw Gretchen and as soon as she had a moment, she rushed over to thank her. Not only had Gretchen done something kind for her, but she had made the festival happen. And it seemed that everyone loved it and couldn't wait for next year.

"I think I'm going to take Orson out of here if you don't mind," she said after a quick hug for Maggie. "He's got himself in another tizzy."

"I heard about Myra," Maggie admitted. "I feel bad for Orson if he's going to be sad living alone, but I wish he was happier for her."

Gretchen offered a small smile. "I think there's more to it than that. When he told me about Brooks and Myra getting engaged, I could tell right away that he was upset she'd be moving out. My first instinct was to invite him to live with me at the bed and breakfast, and well, you can imagine how that went over."

She cackled her reply. "Poor Orson. Not because he'd be living with you, of course. I just mean, he sometimes doesn't handle things very well."

"That's for sure," Gretchen agreed. "Aside from me causing him to nearly hyperventilate, I think he's feeling a little down about the wedding. It sounds like Myra just wanted something small with her and Brooks. Maybe even just at the courthouse."

"Well, if I have anything to say about it, that won't happen. I understand wanting something small, but they have friends here who have become like family, and we want to do something nice for them," Maggie said, getting ahead of herself. Myra hadn't even shared the news officially.

"My point exactly. Orson thinks of Myra like a daughter, and I think it hurt his feelings to know she was happy to be married without him there."

She was starting to understand things now, and she couldn't blame Orson for his feelings, even if he had acted out of turn. Gretchen went off to find Orson and Maggie headed back inside the donut shop, followed by Ruby and the rest of her crew. She was surprised to see Orson already there and was about to tell him Gretchen was looking for him when Brett and Brooks followed everyone inside. She watched as Brooks took his place beside Myra. He nudged her slightly.

"So," Myra began. All faces turned toward her. "There's something we want to share with you."

Orson cleared his throat.

"Brooks asked me to marry him, and I said yes!" Myra squealed, ignoring Orson. Everyone whooped and hugged and congratulated the happy couple. "We want this to happen soon."

"How soon?" Ruby asked.

"In just a few weeks," she answered.

"A few weeks?!" Ruby hooted. "I know we're good, but I don't think we're that good! You really trust us to plan a wedding in that short of a time?"

"Well, we really just want something small…" Myra began.

Ruby clapped her hands. "What about a wedding in a rustic barn on an adorable little farm with a hayride for the bride and groom and a breakfast buffet for the guests? Of course, there will be propane heaters to keep everyone warm just in case the air has a chill."

Myra's mouth gaped open. She cupped her palm over her mouth and tears began to stream down her face. She gazed up at Brooks. "I love it."

"Myra is making me say this part because she was afraid to start crying," he said to a murmur of laughter. "Everyone here knows what brought her to this town. But none of you know what it means to her, to both of us, how you all have become her family since she moved here. You're not only our closest friends, but you're the family she never had before. And the best part about it is that you didn't have to be. You all have loved and supported her just because you wanted to."

"It wasn't hard to do," Ruby added.

"Okay," Myra spoke up next. "I made him do that part so I could get through this part." She took in a long breath and folded her hands in front of her. "You are my family. All of you. I want each and every one of you to be part of the wedding. But the one part of my wedding I didn't want to miss was having someone I love to walk me down the aisle."

Maggie felt the tears well up in her eyes. She glanced at Orson. His face practically shone in pride as he gazed at the couple standing in front of them. He had changed his tune rather quickly when it came down to the real moment.

Myra turned her body and faced him. "I don't have a father to take my arm and walk with me on my wedding day," she said. "So, I am going to ask the man who has been more of a dad to me than any other man my entire life. Orson, would you please take my arm and walk me down the aisle on my wedding day?"

Orson dropped his head and shook it gently side to side. He pulled a white handkerchief out of the back pocket of his pants and wiped his face. When he looked back up to face Myra, his eyes almost glowed. "Of course, I will," he said, then stepped forward to gather her in a tight hug.

Maggie felt the warmth swell over her. After days of feeling the chill of the cold she was overcome by it. Tears ran slowly down her face. She was aware of a light pressure on her hand, and looked down to see a large, chocolate smeared hand covering her own.

Brett stepped in closer and rested his shoulder against hers. Maggie laced her fingers tightly between his and held his hand for as long as the tears in the room continued to flow.

***

If you enjoyed First to Dough, check out the next book in the series, Cake it to Heart, today!

AUTHOR'S NOTE

I'd love to hear your thoughts on my books, the storylines, and anything else that you'd like to comment on —reader feedback is very important to me. My contact information, along with some other helpful links, is listed on the next page. If you'd like to be on my list of "folks to contact" with updates, release and sales notifications, etc.... just shoot me an email and let me know. Thanks for reading!

Also...

... if you're looking for more great reads, Summer Prescott Books publishes several popular series by outstanding Cozy Mystery authors.

CONTACT SUMMER PRESCOTT BOOKS PUBLISHING

Blog and Book Catalog: http://summerprescottbooks.com
Email: summer.prescott.cozies@gmail.com

And...be sure to check out the Summer Prescott Cozy Mysteries fan page and Summer Prescott Books Publishing Page on Facebook – let's be friends!

To sign up for our fun and exciting newsletter, which will give you opportunities to win prizes and swag, enter contests, and be the first to know about New Releases, click here: http://summerprescottbooks.com

Made in United States
North Haven, CT
15 March 2023

34102859R00078